THE TONTO TWO-STEP

SHERRY KENNEY

THE TONTO TWO-STEP

A NOVEL

Hester Press
Denver, Colorado

Published by:

Hester Press
Denver, Colorado
Inquiries: HesterPressCo@gmail.com

Paperback ISBN: 979-8-9868615-1-7
Library of Congress Control Number: 2024919247

Book design: Journey Bound Publishing
Front cover photo: Michael Gallagher
Back cover photo: Gabrielle Col

10 9 8 7 6 5 4 3 2 1
First Edition

*For my women friends—and for those special
men in my life who can be "one of the girls"—
you know who you are.*

The Tonto Two-Step

Dr. Richard Harrington never imagined, in the eighty-three years of his exemplary, though at times sorrowful life, being laid out on an autopsy table, a suspected victim of foul play. But now his body rested in the Maricopa County medical examiner's office in Phoenix, having been exhumed from its grave at Hansen Desert Hills Cemetery in Scottsdale almost three months from the date of his recorded natural death.

PART ONE

One

THE fourteenth of February broke clear and sunny in the Verdes, with expected highs in the seventies, typical weather for the month and the reason people flocked to the area for the winter. Jennifer Crouch started getting ready for the Valentine's Day gala at the Tonto clubhouse while her husband still worked in his home office. As she had explained to him earlier in the day, she was eager to meet people, and wanted to make a good impression tonight. Showered and shampooed, she towel-dried and diffused her hair, using her fingers to style her natural auburn curls. She applied her makeup—according to the lessons she had paid dearly for in Beverly Hills—while still wearing only the lace panties and bra she had recently ordered from the Victoria's Secret online catalogue.

After changing her mind several times, she had settled on a short carmine-red wool and silk blend sheath with a cowl neckline and three-quarter length sleeves. Tasteful, she reminded herself, not too sexy. The crowd would be older, mostly Midwesterners, lots of Lutherans and Disciples of Christ.

John entered the bedroom as Jennifer reached over her shoulder to zip up her dress. He nuzzled her from behind, cupping her breasts in his hands. "Let me help you with that," he murmured into her ear, sliding the zipper in the wrong direction.

"Not now, honey, you'll make us late," she laughed softly, feeling his desire, pleased that she still had this effect on him after thirty years of marriage. He tenderly turned her around and stepped back to admire her, then began undressing for his own quick shower.

"Make me a martini, then?" he said, stepping into a stream of cold water. "My consolation prize?"

Thirty minutes later, she complimented him on his red herringbone-patterned bowtie as he helped her into the car for the short drive to the Tonto Verde clubhouse. Some couples arrived in golf carts, others in cars, and a few, who lived very near, arrived on foot.

Two

"**I** think we're the youngest ones here," Jennifer whispered to John, scanning the scene for a familiar face. She knew they barely qualified to own in this age-restricted community, John having turned fifty-five just six months ago. Many of the residents had been here for decades; they had formed their friendship groups early on. People smiled in their direction, then returned to the conversations they were engaged in.

The clubhouse entrance exploded in a palette of pale and hot pink, crimson, coral, and white. Metallic heart swirl streamers and glittered cutouts hung from the ceiling, while elegant arrangements of tulips, hydrangeas, and ranunculus graced the tables in the Cimarron Dining Room. Servers, with trays of hors d'oeuvres and flutes of champagne, circulated among the handsome couples, taking requests from those who preferred to order a cocktail from the bar.

"I see someone I know…follow me." Relief flooded Jennifer as she led her husband across the room, turning back to ask under her breath, "Are you sure I look okay?"

"You look ravishing, Jeni, really and truly."

Fortified by his reassurance, Jennifer continued her approach to a woman she took to be a youthful sixty-five, who wore a chic black pantsuit trimmed with red silk piping. Her jewelry was silver, contemporary, perhaps acquired from one of the many talented Native American artists in the area.

"Gretchen? I'm Jennifer Crouch. We were in the same putting foursome two Wednesdays ago. What a stunning necklace you're wearing! This is my husband, John."

"Nice to meet you, John. This is my husband, Gary Yarborough. Honey, can you flag down one of those fellows with the bubbly for Jennifer and me?"

While the women sipped champagne and made small talk, the men, who had requested one Scotch rocks and one martini, proceeded to talk about the work they did, or, in Gary's case, had done, before moving from that subject to golf—favorite courses, handicaps, and such—finally agreeing to play together later in the week. As always, Jennifer both envied and admired her husband's easy way with strangers.

"I think they're asking us to sit down to dinner. Shall we look for a table on the patio?" Jennifer invited Gretchen tentatively.

"Yes, let's. It's cool out there, but those overhead heat lamps work well."

The two couples meandered out and sat down, continuing to chat and imbibe as the first course, a demitasse containing French onion soup, arrived. Jennifer made mental notes about the presentation and the recipe, both of which met her approval. The sun gradually melted into the horizon, leaving in its place a colony of voluminous pink clouds tinged with streaks of red.

"What a perfect Valentine's Day sunset," she said. Turning back to Gretchen, she asked, "Did you work, outside the home, I mean?"

"For thirty years, from the time my kids were in school, as a hospice nurse, when hospice was just catching on in the U.S. But when we moved to Arizona ten years ago, I gave it up. It was a fulfilling career, but it took an emotional toll. What about you?"

"I've had various jobs, but nothing I would describe as a career. Before moving here, I worked part time at a boutique in Beverly Hills. Lots of star sightings, very glamourous."

"Well I think some of that glamour rubbed off on you," said Gretchen.

"Oh, thank you, that's very kind." Jennifer glowed at the compliment. "But seriously, I've always wanted to do something meaningful, something that improves people's quality of life. Probably the closest I came was working as an assistant in an attorney's office. She took pro bono cases, women whose children had been removed for neglect. Mostly they were just poor, doing the best they could. Being there to greet them and comfort them felt good. They seemed so sad, or in some cases, angry. But Maryann—my boss—began suffering from depression, because the work demanded so much, with many discouraging results. She started coming in late, looking like she hadn't slept…"

"What happened to her?" Gretchen asked.

"Fortunately, she came from a wonderful family, and they arranged for an intervention. Now she's counsel for a corporation, one of those that's always listed in the top one hundred best places to work. She's married, with two kids—I hear from her every Christmas. That job didn't require much skill beyond listening, but I found it very satisfying."

"Listening is one of the most valuable skills a person can have."

By this time, the empty soup cups had been removed and a chilled salad plate delivered to each place, baby lettuces dressed in a light vinaigrette and garnished with roasted sugared pecans, tart dried cherries, and a crumbling of Roquefort. Jennifer, using the tines of her salad fork, discreetly moved the cheese aside. The sky was dark now, the piano music in the background was moody, and the wine was flowing. Jennifer felt John's gaze on her, and she gave him an encouraging nod.

The meal progressed from the steak and salmon entrée to coffee and flourless chocolate cake and a final round of champagne. By the end of the evening, several couples had stopped by to introduce themselves, and the Crouches had been encouraged to sign up for bridge, and pickleball, and a trivia game night. A few people commented on how the new food and beverage manager had raised the standard for both the service and the food. On the drive home, Jennifer felt exuberant, and her enthusiasm carried over into her lovemaking that night.

Three

THREE days later, John checked in early at the pro shop for a round of golf with Gary Yarborough and two other men, one of whom, Sam Jarvis, he had met briefly at the party on the fourteenth. The fourth golfer introduced himself.

"John, Dick Harrington. Gary tells me you moved recently from California. What do you do? You're too young to be retired."

"Insurance and investments," John said with a laugh. "And you're right, I'm too young to *afford* retirement. What about you?"

"Heart surgeon for thirty years," Dick answered. "Still do a little consulting. My wife and I moved here permanently twenty years ago from the Twin Cities area. Couldn't take the winters anymore. But California…"

"Crazy weather there, too. That, and crazy people."

Fifteen minutes later they were standing at the first tee box.

"Looks like we're up, gentlemen," Sam said. "John, your first time on the Ranch course? Aim for that giant saguaro. It's a layup to the edge of one of those darned gulches that run through here."

"Don't worry, you won't make it, no matter how good you are," said Gary. "From there you can see the pin."

Four hours and a few minutes later, they cleared the eighteenth green, making plans to continue their conversation—which had turned to the price of real estate in the East Valley—over lunch at a table in the Mesquite Grill.

"The problem is water, of course, which is why we're here in the Verdes. But the assurance of having it has really driven home prices up here," said Sam. "We were lucky to discover this place years ago. How did you find it, John?"

"Through a client, in a way," John said. "I came for a meeting in DC Ranch last fall, and he and his wife brought Jennifer and me out to Tonto Verde for dinner one night. The restaurant still opened to the public at that time. The grounds and the views were so spectacular, we drank the Kool-Aid. Came back with a real estate agent the next day.

"So far, we couldn't be happier with the decision to move. But you're right about the prices. That, and low inventory. Our Realtor advised us to offer at least five percent over asking. I doubt ours was even the highest offer our sellers received, but some of the others were from investors, and this couple didn't want to do that to their neighbors.

"I guess there's a huge market for short term rentals in the area," he added, referring to the exorbitant rents charged during the Waste Management Phoenix Open in February, and Major League Baseball spring training, which began a few weeks later.

"Anyway, here we are, in a condo, for now. My plan is to move us into a house, hopefully with a view of Four Peaks, as soon as possible. My wife has her heart set on it. As they say, happy wife, happy life…"

"The Tonto two-step," said Gary. Sam and Dick smiled, and nodded in agreement.

The men signed their tabs and headed out, John in his car and the others in their carts, having made plans for their next round together the following week.

Four

"HOW did you play?" Jennifer asked, as John stopped to remove his shoes by the garage door.

"Okay, I guess, and with a great group of guys." He crossed the kitchen and planted a kiss on her forehead. "Their regular fourth just moved back to Michigan, so I'm in. We should plan a dinner party so you can meet the other two wives. You know Gary's already."

"Honey, I'm not sure we can seat eight people around this table," she hedged, glancing toward the dining room. The table gleamed, its fine-grained wooden base polished to perfection, with a glass top that showcased the rug beneath it. Besides their bed, it was the first good piece of furniture they had bought after marrying, paying it off in installments for over a year. Jennifer had agreed to leave many of their old belongings behind in California, but the table she insisted on bringing.

"It isn't the table, really," she laughed. "It's getting eight chairs around it and not having our guests feel like they're in a can of sardines."

"Happy hour, then, and our guests can stand—just kidding! You're too beautiful and too good a cook for me not to want to show you off, Jeni. Look, I need to clean up and check my mail, then maybe I'll listen to sports and close my eyes for a few minutes."

"You do your thing; I have plenty to keep me busy." Jennifer gave him a wink. "That's not actually true, but I'm working on it."

Once John finished napping, they went out for a walk around the neighborhood. They were passing a beautiful property on Palo Fiero, across from one of the few remaining undeveloped lots in Tonto Verde, when John waved an older man over.

"Dick," John said. "This is my wife, Jennifer. Jeni, I played golf with Dick today."

"Nice to meet you." Jennifer smiled, as she and Dick shook hands. "I hear it was a nice round."

Dick laughed. "Great day and great company, but my game's not what it used to be."

"I disagree. That putt you made on nine was terrific," John said.

While the men revisited their round, Jennifer took in her surroundings. The Spanish-style stucco and tile-roofed home had a footprint of at least four thousand square feet. The perfectly manicured rockscape was accented with cacti not yet in bloom, including pin cushions, prickly pears, and cereus. Two mature Blue Palo Verdes provided privacy and shade, and a low stone wall with a weathered iron gate enclosed a small courtyard where flowering succulents cascaded from their planters. A lump of longing tinged with envy rose in Jennifer's throat.

"Do you have time for a beer?" Dick asked.

Jennifer gave John a nod and they followed their host through the open gate and up a flagstone path.

The Harrigans' stunning view began at the front door and continued straight through an open floor plan and a wall of sliding glass doors. The expanse of the Peaks course and the Mazatzal mountain range beyond took Jennifer's breath away.

"Gorgeous," she said, although the word hardly did the panorama justice.

"Ah, my better half," Dick said, as a petite, silver-haired woman approached them.

"Shirley Harrington," she said, extending her tiny hand first to Jennifer, and then to John. "I'm drinking chardonnay; may I pour you a glass, or would you prefer a cocktail?"

"Wine would be lovely, thank you," replied Jennifer.

Dick put his arm around John's shoulder in male comradery. "Beer or wine for you, or something stronger?"

"Beer, please," responded John. With the ease of a practiced host, Dick removed a cold glass mug from a stainless-steel Sub Zero and emptied a bottle of Michelob into it.

"Let's go outside and take in the view," Dick suggested.

There were multiple seating arrangements on the spacious patio, but Dick led them to a shady area on one end that featured a love seat, and two chairs, grouped in a semi-circle around a coffee table. The furniture was constructed of sturdy metal with a lattice design. The slightly sun-bleached cushions were a retro forties print, their floral theme echoed in the huge, glazed palm-filled ceramic pots spaced artfully around the exterior space. On the opposite end of the patio, a sheet of water fell dramatically over an elevated wall to a shimmering infinity pool below. Jennifer couldn't help wondering what the couple had done before retirement. Money, it seemed, was no object.

Shirley soon joined them, carrying a tray of small delicacies—niçoise olives, marcona almonds, and sliced figs at the perfect point of ripeness. Jennifer studied her as she placed it on the coffee table before them. Early eighties, delicate bone structure under clear, finely wrinkled porcelain skin, and deep-set blue eyes that seemed to emanate acceptance, and another emotion Jennifer couldn't quite identify.

"To the Crouches," said Dick, lifting his glass as his wife sat down next to him. "Welcome to the Verdes. We've been coming here since Day One, knew the family that developed both Rio and Tonto, from Minnesota. We bought a lot when they were cheap and built this house; finally moved here full-time when I retired from surgery. It's a special place. We hope you'll love it as much as we do.

"Of course, the summers months are hot, and getting hotter every year. That's when we travel to cooler climes, fish with friends in Montana and Idaho, Colorado sometimes. Go to the opera in Santa Fe. We're lucky to have friends with homes in prime places. We reciprocate by inviting them here in the winter."

"Tell us about yourself, Jennifer," steered Shirley. "Are you a golfer?"

"No, I'm not, but I haven't ruled out the possibility of taking it up. I putt with the ladies on Wednesdays, mostly to meet people, but I may buy a set of clubs and sign up for lessons. I had a small garden in California, and I worked part-time. I can't easily do those things here, so I'm trying to reinvent myself. I'm learning bridge and pickleball, and I read. And I try to make myself work out at the fitness center several times a week."

"Well," said Shirley, "you sound busy, but I would love to have you join me next Tuesday morning over at the church in Rio Verde, making sandwiches for La Casita. It's a program in Fountain Hills that helps families who have experienced hardship get back on their feet. It's a nice group that shows up on Tuesdays, mostly women but a few men, too, and the cause is worthwhile. You'll like the pastor; she's an attractive woman about your age.

"And what about you, John?" Shirley continued.

"My work is insurance and investments, doctor clients mostly, in the Los Angeles area. But I've connected with a firm in Scottsdale that I'll be meeting with next week. Fingers crossed I'll soon be developing more business closer to our new home. I'm also looking forward to regular golf with Dick; he has quite a game."

"He's always enjoyed it," agreed Shirley. "I gave it up several years ago, but we played some beautiful courses together, every one of them a bird sanctuary. That's the main attraction for me."

The sun had set, and the time had come to thank their hosts and say goodnight. Plans were confirmed for the following week—golf for the men, sandwich-making for the women. The stars began appearing overhead, and Jennifer glowed as she and John left through the side gate and resumed their walk toward home.

Five

"**THEY** seem like a nice young couple," said Shirley, as she carried the tray of empty dishes inside. Removing a cold chicken breast from the refrigerator, she sliced it thinly and arranged it across a bed of mixed greens, drizzling a light dressing over the salad and garnishing it with halved cherry tomatoes and Persian cucumber discs. After adding a grinding of black pepper, she carried the plate to the table, where her husband had set two places and poured two half glasses of an Alexander Valley pinot noir.

"Artfully done, as always," Dick complimented, as he pulled her chair from the table and stood until she sat. After his brief blessing, she resumed the line of conversation she had begun.

"It's hard to make new friends here, I suspect. Everyone is cordial, of course, but we all have our groups. It isn't snobbishness, just laziness, perhaps."

"My wife, a one-woman welcome wagon," smiled Dick. "And I love her dearly," he added.

"And you do love your alliteration," she smiled.

"Indeed I do. By the way, what time are we expected at the Yarboroughs' tomorrow? Maybe they've included the Crouches—Gary's the one who invited John to join our foursome."

"Five-thirty, with appetizers. And that would be nice, I hope they'll be there. In any event, I'll make sure Jennifer meets some new people next week. Volunteering is a great way to connect."

After dinner, Shirley cleared the table and loaded the dishwasher. Dick offered to help but she shooed him away. "Turn on the fireplace," she suggested, "and let's read for a while." By the time she sat down, he was in his recliner, thumbing through the latest issue of the *American Journal of Cardiology*. She turned on the floor lamp next to her overstuffed armchair, and picked up a hardcover copy of *This is Happiness*, a book by Niall Williams she had borrowed from a friend. As she read, she fondled the soft edges of a small, multi-colored quilt that she had draped over her legs.

"I can't stay awake another minute," Dick said. Shirley closed her book after marking her place, and took the hand he offered her. She turned her face toward his, tears glistening in her eyes. They moved as one toward the bedroom, Dick turning out the lights as they went.

Six

THE following Monday morning, John Crouch backed his car out of the garage at eight o'clock and pulled away from his home. He turned onto Agua Verde, the street that encircled the mid-perimeter of the Tonto Verde community, and then onto Tonto Verde Drive. Waiting patiently at the exit gates, he could almost hear them creaking, though his windows were raised and the radio on. He turned left onto Forest Road and left again onto Rio Verde Drive, setting the cruise control in his BMW X1 for five miles above the posted speed limits of forty, then fifty, driving west toward Scottsdale Boulevard.

John had been invited to attend a nine o'clock meeting at the offices of McDougal Partners, a boutique wealth management firm he was introduced to while still living in California. One of his doctor clients there had retired to Arizona, met the McDougal brothers on the golf course, and one thing led to another. John was grateful for the contact. He made his way through a stretch of road construction and entered the parking lot of a small commercial office complex that matched the address he had put into his GPS. After wrestling a reflective sunshade into place on the car's dash, he headed into the building that bore the McDougal name.

A tall, buxom blonde John assessed to be early twenty-something sat behind the reception desk. She greeted him when he gave her his name and led him to a conference room. It opened to an interior courtyard, where miniature palm trees and vibrant succulents in terracotta pots surrounded a fountain constructed of native limestone.

"Would you like something to drink, Mr. Crouch?" the young woman asked. "A cup of coffee, or perhaps something cool?" She indicated a credenza with two trays, one holding a coffee maker and mugs, the other a pitcher of filtrated water, glasses, an ice bucket, and a variety of flavored sparkling waters in colorful cans.

"Just water, please, no ice." Once she'd handed him the drink, he walked to the windows opposite the courtyard to take in the view. On the near horizon, private jets took off from and landed at Scottsdale Airport, carrying wealthy executives, professionals, and entrepreneurs to and from conferences, or ski trips or golf outings disguised as conferences. He had read that nearby Paradise Valley, a Phoenix suburb in the heart of Scottsdale, had the highest net worth per capita of any U.S. municipality, with its neighboring zip codes coming in second and third.

Four more men trickled in, and John introduced himself to each of them in turn, curious to learn why they had all been invited to what he'd assumed was a private interview. Finally, Stephen McDougal, who had extended the invitations, came into the room, poured himself a cup of coffee, and shook hands with John and the others before inviting them to sit.

Stephen's brother, James, entered at precisely nine o'clock, closing the door behind him and taking a seat at the head of the rectangular conference table. He was clearly the elder McDougal, tall and distinguished looking, his full head of hair graying at the temples, his skin tanned. He wore a lightweight, wool blend sport jacket over an open-collared Eton shirt. Pressed khaki pants, hemmed to the perfect length, broke slightly over the Ferragamo loafers he wore with thin dress socks.

"I'm glad you're all here," began James, "and I hope you'll linger after our little chat and continue becoming acquainted. Each of you comes highly recommended, either by one of our clients, or by one of yours. I'll get right to the point. Our firm," he nodded toward his brother, "has developed more business than it can comfortably handle. We're leaving money on the table, and we don't like doing that. So we've decided to triple the number of associates in our organization.

"The potential for encountering wealth here, and for building it for our clients and ourselves, is staggering. The business model we're known for is both high tech and high touch. Our products are proprietary, designed by some of the best fund managers and insurance companies in the world.

"We've run background checks on each of you. We require signed and notarized confidentiality and non-compete agreements. The clients belong to the company. Compensation is salary plus production bonuses. Benefits are good. Expense accounts are generous—car leases, club dues, that kind of thing. We like to entertain our clients and their spouses in style, but not in an overly lavish manner. Optics matter. Steve here will answer any questions you have. Think it over and let us know within a week."

And with that James McDougal exited the room as abruptly as he had entered it.

Seven

"**HOW** did it go?" Jennifer asked, when John entered their condo through the garage door at noon.

"Interesting," he replied. "It's a good opportunity, but there's a downside. I wouldn't be building my own book of business; I'd be building theirs. The McDougal brothers obviously intend to grow their firm and then sell it to some hedge fund for a fortune, and who knows when that might happen? I don't like the idea of giving up control over my future.

"But the money's good. There's something to be said for a predictable income after years of working on straight commission, with someone else picking up the tab for health insurance. And they take care of expenses." John shrugged. "I don't know, Jeni, I need to think. If you haven't eaten, I'll buy you lunch."

Jennifer responded by putting on a hat and her sunglasses and heading for the front door. They cut through the neighborhood and walked the path around the lake, admiring a snowy egret, poised like a statue, at its edge. Entering the clubhouse through the bar, they reminded Sandy, the young woman who greeted them, of their names and member number. She invited them to take any table.

"Tell me about *your* morning," John said, when they were settled next to each other on a banquette at the back of the bar, two icy Arnold Palmers in front of them.

"Uneventful," she said. "Shirley Harrington called to say she'll pick me up tomorrow to go to the church. She'll be in our driveway at nine."

Their food arrived, a burger for John and a Cobb salad for her, half of which she planned to take home in a to-go box. Despite John's earlier chattiness, he fell into a silence Jennifer chose not to interrupt. After three decades of marriage, she recognized those times when her husband needed to be alone with his thoughts.

The next morning, she woke early and was surprised to find John up before her, drinking coffee at the dining room table, surrounded by pencil, ledger paper, and his financial calculator. Though he had mastered Microsoft Excel in business school, when things were critical, he reverted to an old-fashioned spreadsheet.

"My question is," she heard him mutter as she poured herself a cup, "how long will it be before they sell the business? If the money's as good as they say, five to seven years may be all I need."

She kissed the top of his head and pulled out the chair next to him while he continued, meeting her eyes. "If we could just go back in time, Jeni, if I could just have a do-over…"

His moan of regret was all too familiar. Jennifer never knew whether to ignore it, or to offer sympathy. She had resolved her own disappointment years ago, without ever accusing or criticizing her husband. As far as she was concerned, what had happened was now water under the bridge.

Shirley Harrington arrived at the appointed time, and in just a few minutes, they reached Christ Church in the Desert, just a few miles down the road. There, in the fellowship hall, a group of church members had arranged large quantities of ham, turkey, and cheese slices, lettuce and tomatoes, and white and whole wheat rolls.

"Hi Shirley," several people exclaimed as the two entered, adding welcoming nods or a "hello" when they spotted Jennifer. She and Shirley each found a place in the assembly line and joined in making small talk and sandwiches.

"How's Dick?" one of the women asked Shirley. "Still enjoying his golf?"

"He plays several times a week," Shirley responded, "but he seems to need a longer soak in the spa afterwards these days. What about Jim?"

"Same thing. Getting old is not for sissies, as my dad used to say. We just feel lucky to be alive, and to be enjoying our children and grand–…" the woman stopped short.

"It's okay, Kristina," said Shirley, "I understand how dear grandchildren are, and I am happy for you, and for all my friends who have been blessed with them."

In the awkward silence that followed, Jennifer realized she didn't know whether Shirley had children or not. But the conversations slowly resumed, and soon one hundred sandwiches had been assembled and packed for delivery.

"That was fun," Jennifer commented to Shirley, as they left the church.

"Shall we extend our time together over lunch?"

"That would be nice."

There were several small groups of women already dining when they arrived back at Tonto Verde and were shown to a table on the clubhouse patio. Shirley made brief introductions as they passed by;

though, she explained to Jennifer when they were seated, she had trouble remembering some of the newer residents' names.

After placing their orders, Shirley asked Jennifer, "Is there anything new in your lives?"

"A little. John's meeting in Scottsdale yesterday went well. He just needs to decide if the organization is right for him. The compensation package is generous, but there's no opportunity for ownership, and John is very entrepreneurial. And he's concerned about the McDougals' trajectory, concerned about having enough time to make up for past losses."

Darn it, Jennifer, too much information.

"I'm sorry Shirley, I'm sure that's more than you care to know about our personal situation."

"Actually dear, I'm interested, and I'm happy you feel you can trust me with the details. I understand they're confidential."

"Thank you, you're very kind. John has a week to make up his mind, so prayers for discernment are appreciated."

"I'll put that one at the top of my list."

As they pulled into Jennifer's driveway, Shirley asked, "Shall we do this again next week?"

"I'd like that," Jennifer answered, thrilled to accept the invitation. "Thank you, Shirley," she said, as she exited the car and waved goodbye.

John, beer in hand, joined her on the patio later that afternoon, where she sat sipping a glass of wine and listening to smooth jazz on a small speaker, the volume turned low. This was her favorite time of day.

Two cardinals flitted among the trees that separated the Crouches from their neighbors on each side, occasionally dropping to the ground to pick up a seed or an invisible insect. Several pairs of doves made their mournful call. The sun sank low on the horizon, its brilliance reflected onto a bank of clouds to the southwest. A small aircraft zigzagged across the desert beyond, it's vrooms and hums fading in and out. Soon the coyotes would begin to howl.

"This is so peaceful, so relaxing," said Jennifer.

"But temporary," John assured her. "This small patio, I mean, and this view. I know what you want, Jeni, and I'm going to get it for you. Now, tell me about your time with Shirley."

"Delightful! I really enjoy her company, even though she's old enough to be my mother. She knows everyone, and it's clear she's loved and respected in this community. I wonder if she's just being nice to me because I'm new."

"Not because you're new, because you're you. You're fun to be with, Jeni."

"That's easy for *you* to say."

"Yes, it is." He reached for her hand and squeezed it. "I talked to Steve McDougal today, expressed my concerns. He convinced me they have no immediate plans to sell the company."

"That's good news."

"He went on to emphasize that their prospect list is long and promising, and said they knew I would be successful working it. When I need to go back to California to service my clients, the firm will cover the cost. The only problem is that any new business, even with my existing clients, belongs to them. But if my math is right, it's still a net win for us. I'm going in tomorrow to sign a contract. Steve also gave me the contact for their auto leasing agent, told me to select a new car, high end but not too showy, so you get the BMW back. That should make you happy."

"You know it does, honey. In fact, that calls for another glass of wine."

Eight

THE Lady Putters gathered on Wednesday mornings. They signed in at the registration table and learned which hole they were to start on, then stood in clusters with their friends and chatted until the game of the day was announced. Jennifer dreaded this standing around time and had developed the habit of scanning the group for the paper nametags that indicated new members. She moved directly toward these women, hoping they were also there to make new friends.

The women were encouraged to wear blue. This morning, Jennifer made a mental note to order an official, branded blue shirt or jacket in the pro shop. She didn't really need anything new just for putting, but maybe it would make her feel more like an insider. She had become a decent putter, since joining the group at the beginning of the year, by watching YouTube clips and practicing—during the week by herself, and on the weekend with John. She had even taken home some meager winnings, which she kept in an envelope on the kitchen counter, teasing her husband that she would buy him a drink at the bar when she had accumulated enough money.

After their rounds, the foursomes sat together around eight-tops in a small private dining room, with a buffet lunch set up in the middle. Today, Jennifer sat next to a woman named Marty, and casually shared her volunteer experience of the previous day, mentioning Shirley by name.

"Do you know Shirley's history?" Marty asked, in a low voice.

"Not really," responded Jennifer cautiously, "we've only recently met. I know she and Dick moved from Minnesota to be here fulltime, after coming out for years."

"Yes," said Marty. "They were among the first to build. They moved permanently after their young adult son died. It's been over twenty years, but…"

"That's terrible," murmured Jennifer. "I…" she hesitated. "I thought I sensed something, something like grief, or maybe resignation, the first time I met her. And then yesterday, at the church, there was this curious conversation. Does she talk about it?"

"Never."

The luncheon continued. Winners were announced and prizes awarded, but Jennifer's mind had wandered. There was a part of her that wished Marty hadn't shared this sad story about her new friend. She hated the thought of knowing it, but not letting on to Shirley that she knew.

She retrieved her putter as soon as it felt socially acceptable to leave, and slowly walked the longer route back to the condominium.

Nine

DEPUTY Sheriff Frank Chavez pulled into the parking lot at the District Seven office in Fountain Hills and exited the black SUV assigned to him. The vehicle featured a picture of the Maricopa County sheriff's badge on both driver and passenger sides, with "Sheriff" emblazoned in large gold decaled letters. He entered the building and tipped his hat to the woman sitting at the bullet-proof-glass-protected reception desk, unlocking the door beyond and heading toward the kitchenette.

"What's happening?" Frank set a cup of hot coffee down on the dispatcher's desk a few minutes later, and sat to face him.

"Not much, sir. No suspected human trafficking, no overnight property break-ins, no reported drug deals, not even a rattlesnake curled up in a patio pot."

"Let's keep it that way, son."

"I'll do my best, sir."

Frank headed toward his office, leaving the door open, per his policy. He then leaned back in his chair and listened to voicemail messages play through the speakerphone while his computer booted up for email.

Someone had sent him a picture of a pick-up truck with two huge American flags flying from the tailgate and the words "Let's go Brandon" printed on the back windshield. "Isn't there something you can do about this?" read the sender's message. He responded, "No ma'am, I'm sorry, this is an expression of free speech." He was just grateful the reports of stolen yard signs from the recent hotly contested gubernatorial election had died down, as had the shouting matches in the We-Ko-Pa Casino Resort parking lot, over whether the 2020 presidential election had been stolen.

All in all, it was a calm day in a beautiful desert setting—a certified dark sky community located due east of Scottsdale, named for the fountain in the middle of the man-made lake in the center of town.

Frank, originally christened Francisco, had grown up north of Chicago, where Latinos had not been as integrated into the population as they were here in the Southwest. Not that he hadn't experienced discrimination here—he had—but he hadn't experienced the hatred he'd sometimes felt growing up. This reached its lowest point when he and two friends were picked up after attending a basketball game in their high school gym. They never learned why they'd been picked up. "Walking while being brown", they'd later quipped. They'd been handcuffed and pushed into the back seat of a cop car, driven around town in bursts of speed alternated with sudden stops, while they banged back and forth between the seat and the plexiglass shield that divided them from their tormentors.

This experience might have caused him to hate the police and rebel against the system. Instead, Francisco vowed to become a different kind of cop. He applied to study criminal justice at the University of

Arizona in Tucson and received a scholarship, changing his name to Frank when he made the move.

He never returned to the home he had grown up in. After his graduation, he moved his mother and his younger sister, Maria, to Arizona. Maria had attended Arizona State University, studied nursing, passed her boards, and gone to work at the Mayo Clinic in Scottsdale, where she was now Head Nurse Supervisor in the Department of Cardiovascular Medicine.

Their mother, Aurelia, lived with Frank and his wife Margaret, whom he had met on a blind date in college. Their twin daughters, Scottie and Ginny, were born early in the marriage, and Frank woke up happy almost every day in a small but charming adobe-style home in the hills, surrounded by four adoring females. Maria, who also idolized him, lived just a few miles away.

After touching base with the deputies under his command, Frank went out on patrol. The slogan "Integrity, Accountability & Community" printed on the flanks of his truck were words he took to heart. Fountain Hills was, by all accounts, a desirable place to live, and very safe compared to other parts of the Phoenix metropolitan area, but Frank knew it could always be better.

At the southwest corner of Shea and Fountain Hills boulevards, Frank rolled down his window to say "hello" to a man in dreadlocks who sat on the curb, his possessions held close in a black garbage bag. Jessie was a known entity in Fountain Hills, and though the major intersections in town all posted signs that discouraged giving to panhandlers, the residents gave to him regularly.

Jessie's story pretty much checked off every stereotypical box for single men experiencing homelessness. He was bipolar, grew up in foster care, dropped out of high school, volunteered for the war in Iraq, came back with PTSD, couldn't find work, and got into street drugs. He'd told Frank the whole sad story one day, and Frank suggested the man try the Veteran's Administration or a shelter in Phoenix, offering to transport him personally. But Jessie preferred the landscape, and the people, of Fountain Hills.

Frank turned right onto Fountain Hills Boulevard and drove back through town, past the Burger King and the Safeway and through the intersection at Palisades Boulevard to the edge of town, into McDowell Mountain Park toward the Verdes. Bikers favored the winding two-lane road that ran through the park, with its posted speed limit of forty-five. Most locals observed it, or at least held themselves to five to ten miles above it, but some drivers insisted on going sixty, and when the slower drivers held them back, resorted to passing. This was the violation Frank most objected to, as it simultaneously put bikers in danger of being run off the road, and oncoming traffic at risk of a head-on collision. When he pulled someone over for speeding, he typically issued a warning. But when he caught a driver coming around a curve, passing at high speed, he did not let them off that easy.

He reached the intersection at Forest Road, where the only option was a left-hand turn, the Yavapai pecan orchards stretching ahead and to the right for as far as one could see. He made the turn and continued north, past Rio Verde, then Tonto Verde, to the stop sign at the intersection with Rio Verde Drive. He considered stopping at O'Dogz, the food truck regularly parked there and frequented by workers and residents alike, but he wasn't yet hungry for lunch. So he turned left and proceeded past the burgeoning Trilogy community on the right. As he headed toward North Scottsdale, Rio Verde Drive converting to Dynamite Road along the way, he acknowledged—not for the first time—that he was basically driving a big square around the desert, but he never tired of the route.

Ten

JENNIFER'S phone rang early on the last Tuesday in May, just as she took the final sip of coffee from her first cup.

"Good morning, Shirley" she answered cheerfully, before processing how unusual it was to be receiving a phone call at seven a.m. "I really meant to call yesterday to tell you again how much we enjoyed the drive to Sedona with you and Dick over the weekend. Such a lovely respite from the heat!"

"We enjoyed it too, dear, and we hope to do it again soon. But Jennifer, I'm not feeling well this morning," the older woman continued, her voice barely audible. "Please go to the church without me today."

"What is it, Shirley? Have you seen a doctor?" Jennifer asked, forgetting, in the moment, that her friend was married to one.

"Dick may take me over to the clinic in Scottsdale later," Shirley answered. "I have a headache, fever and chills. It's probably the flu, but not COVID; I took a test."

"I'm so sorry you aren't feeling well. I'll let everyone know. Please rest up and get better soon. And let me know what I can pick up for you. I'm going into town today. In fact, please count on me to bring dinner to you and Dick."

"That would be nice, dear. I don't have any appetite, but Dick needs his strength. I'll tell him. He'll be grateful, and I am, too."

When John came into the kitchen, fresh from the shower and smelling faintly of the lime-scented aftershave lotion he had worn since she met him, Jennifer told him about the call. He poured a cup of coffee and joined her at the table.

"I'm worried. Shirley sounded so weak. We've become so close; I sometimes forget she's thirty years older than I am. I don't know what I would do if anything happened to her."

"Our older friends will probably go before we do, Jeni, that's just the way it is. Imagine how hard it would be for Shirley if something happened to you first. But she'll be fine. According to Dick, they're both in good health, and they have ready access to experts in every sub-specialty at the Mayo. Try not to worry. You're sweet to take food.

"Now, I need to head out. I have a breakfast meeting, then golf at The Camelback with some IT execs. I'll be home in time for cocktails. Make a dinner reservation if you like, okay?"

Jennifer rose to kiss him goodbye. What began as a quick brush of her lips against his lingered, and deepened, until he reluctantly pulled away.

Eleven

JENNIFER dressed for the day in light blue denim capris and a white knit top, pulling her curly hair into a high ponytail and tying a small, square, red and white polka-dotted scarf around it. Tinted sunscreen, a touch of mascara, some lipstick, and she was ready to go. Since she and Shirley would not be riding together to Rio Verde, Jennifer planned to volunteer at the church and then drive directly into Fountain Hills for groceries. She grabbed her shopping bags and headed back to the table for the list she had been making when Shirley called that morning. After the call, Jennifer had added the ingredients for a hot chicken salad—her go-to casserole—and lasagna, a recipe she planned to double.

She drove the thirty-five mile-per-hour speed limit toward Rio Verde, arriving at the church in four minutes. Christ Church in the Desert, a non-denominational, Protestant congregation, was home to many of the Christians in the adjoining Verdes communities. The church offered an associate membership to those whose primary membership was elsewhere.

Visitors were made to feel welcome, and Jennifer and John had worshipped there on a semi-regular basis since becoming friends with the Harringtons, after which the four of them would typically go back to the Cimarron Dining Room for Sunday brunch. There were very few young people in the church, though the youth population grew during spring breaks and holidays, when children and grand-children visited. Jennifer and John had never been church-goers, but she found the experience both stimulating and soothing, and John seemed to agree. She had even broached the question of their joining the church and was pleased when he hadn't objected.

The group gathered today greeted Jennifer warmly when she walked into the fellowship hall across the breezeway from the sanctuary. Someone asked, "Where's Shirley?"

"She's ill," Jennifer explained. "She called me early this morning, and to be honest, she sounded terrible. She described her symptoms to me. It sounds like the flu. I'm taking dinner over later today."

"That's awful," a woman named Sue lamented, "and after getting past COVID. We should have all kept wearing our masks, I guess, except I am so over that!" Everyone nodded their heads in agree-ment. Then they set about the task at hand, finishing in less than two hours. Pastor Jean offered a short prayer for Shirley and asked Jennifer to check back in with her after delivering the meal, adding that she would call Dick tomorrow for an update and would let the group know of any developments. Jennifer felt better when she left than when she had arrived, her spirit lifted by the companionship of others who shared her affection for her friend.

Leaving the Verdes, Jennifer set her cruise control at fifty for the drive through the desert park, streaming Taylor Swift through the car's speakers, intent on sustaining the good mood she had worked herself into. Thank goodness John had gotten his new car, an Audi A6 in a classy, blue-grey color, with a trunk large enough for two sets of clubs. Sharing one car for even a short time had been a bit inconvenient, though rarely a real problem. The second car they had left behind in California wasn't worth bringing. Now she had the BMW for herself, and she liked the feeling of independence.

She passed the pull-off where the local sheriff's deputy sometimes parked. He sat there today, radar gun pointed at oncoming traffic. She tapped her brakes and gave him a smile and a little wave. She and John had once seen him helping to change a tire on an old pick-up truck transporting a group of laborers.

"He's a good guy," they had told each other, and articles in the *Fountain Hills Times* had confirmed their first impression.

Jennifer knew her way around the grocery store and walked the aisles at a quick pace, choosing what she needed for the casseroles, including disposable pans, and replenishing the staples she and John were running low on. She had heard the women in Tonto Verde joke about texting their friends from the grocery store to see if anyone needed anything. She wasn't that close to anyone but Shirley, and the thought caused a tiny pang of anxiety. "Shake it off, shake it off," she sang softly to herself.

When she returned home, she unloaded her groceries and went to work. Surveying her small but efficient kitchen, she declared aloud, "This is my kingdom—I rule this space."

Growing up with two working parents, she had routinely prepared their meals from the time she could open the refrigerator door. Neither her mom nor her dad had earned a diploma, though he eventually received a GED, and their jobs had combined long hours with low pay. They'd struggled to make ends meet, moving often from one rental to another. There was no money for music lessons or sports uniforms. In her youth, Jennifer Johnson had walked straight home from school each day, focused on staying out of trouble, making decent grades, and getting creative with the meager supplies in their pantry long before "food insecurity" became a commonly used term.

More than one of Jennifer's high school teachers had encouraged her to learn a foreign language and to challenge her intellectual ability with advanced science and math courses. Instead, she'd studied home economics—learning to plan menus, create household budgets, and sew her own clothes, using one of the machines at school. During the spring semester of her junior year, the guidance counselor invited her into his office, asking if she had thought about attending college, affirming she had the ability to succeed, and perhaps to obtain an academic scholarship in addition to financial aid. But Jennifer couldn't visualize it. The most positive picture she could evoke for her future was one that included graduating, finding a job, and renting her own apartment.

That first apartment, though tiny, had been her little corner of heaven, especially when she met John Crouch the very same week she moved in, at a Friday night poolside mixer. John was five years her senior, a recent graduate of UCLA's business school. He had turned down multiple recruiting offers with well-known firms to go to work for an insurance company, on straight commission. He had explained to Jennifer, "I'm not afraid of hard work, and I don't want limits on what I can earn. And, I like being my own boss."

John's easy-going personality attracted people to him; he seemed to Jennifer to be a natural salesman. Back then, he'd worked fourteen-hour days, cold-calling prospects in the beginning, then following up on the numerous referrals he received as he developed a loyal clientele. Many weekdays, every meal involved a client meeting, a calorie intake John balanced with regular early morning runs. Jennifer knew some girls would have written off a man with so little time to share, but she had admired John's ambition, encouraged his efforts, and celebrated his successes.

They'd established a routine that involved her cooking dinner for him on Friday nights—every week a little anniversary. After working all day on Saturdays, he would take her out, often surprising her with a new restaurant—one reputed to be impossible to get into—or a cultural or sports event for which he had gotten tickets. During the week, Jennifer loved anticipating the gourmet meal she would prepare for John, and the interesting adventure he would have planned for her. Their romance blossomed, slowly at first, and then with an intensity that made it hard for either of them to concentrate on anything except each other. A year after meeting, they drove down to the courthouse on Cesar Chavez Avenue, obtained a California marriage license, and within an hour became husband and wife.

Twelve

JENNIFER prepared her casseroles in the disposable pans and paired them with bags of fresh greens. She added a few small containers of homemade dressing, as well as mini baguettes she had sliced, buttered, and wrapped in foil. She had baked a recipe of brownies, and she pulled a quart of sea salt caramel ice cream from the freezer at the last minute, placing it in an insulated bag to add to the box she'd loaded in her car for the drive to the Harringtons.

Dick met Jennifer at the front door. He wore a medical mask, and offered one to her, as he took the large box of food from her arms.

"You're a saint," he said. "Let's put these things in the kitchen; then we can go outside and sit under the misters, and I'll give you an update." He poured Jennifer a glass of white wine, picked up a half empty bottle of beer from the countertop, and led the way through the sliding glass door, indicating a chair for her that maximized the spectacular view.

"Shirley is being kept overnight for observation", he said, removing his mask. "We think it may be Valley fever, but it's too soon to say for sure. The symptoms present like several other diagnoses. Fortunately, the clinic has a team of specialists who deal with this, and a center devoted to it in Phoenix. They treat around fifteen hundred patients a year with the disease."

"Valley fever? I've never heard of it," said Jennifer. "Is it contagious? How did Shirley get it?"

"It isn't contagious," Dick answered. "It's an infection of the lungs, contracted by breathing one of two cocci fungi that live in the soil in our desert. Chances are that all the construction in the area, coupled with the high winds we've been having, are the cause. In healthy people, it normally resolves itself, sometimes with the aid of an anti-fungal medication. Shirley's healthy, but age is also a factor, which is one of the reasons we decided it best to keep her under observation. That, and the fact that she's feeling so weak."

"Can she have visitors?"

"I know Shirley would love to see you, Jennifer; she's very fond of you, and your visit would be a comfort. Why don't I call you tomorrow morning when I get to the clinic? I'll learn more about what tests they plan to give her, whether they'll be keeping her there or sending her home, and so on."

He nodded at the house. "My big decision at this point is whether to have lasagna or chicken tonight. Whichever it is I know it will be delicious. After dinner I plan to go right to bed—I didn't get much sleep last night."

Thirteen

JENNIFER made the drive home slowly, taking in the beauty and the amenities surrounding her—the clubhouse, the putting green, and the bocce courts. She looked out over the lake, where multiple duck families dove and dabbled for food, and admired the colorful desert landscape around it, dotted by thirty-six immaculately groomed holes of golf beyond. She could hardly believe the good fortune she and John had in discovering this community. She loved everything about this place, except for the nagging sense that she didn't quite belong. "Why this insecurity?" she chided herself in a quiet voice. "You have as much right as anyone else to be here."

When she pulled into the driveway and pressed the garage door opener, she saw the Audi already parked inside.

"Honey, I'm so happy you're home," she said, rushing to her husband.

"Hey, babe," he said, taking her in his arms. "May I pour you a glass of wine?"

"Please," she answered, staying right where she was for a minute longer.

They sat close together on the sofa, the television tuned to the golf channel—muted—while she told John the little she knew about Shirley's condition.

"I refuse to google Valley fever," she concluded, "even though I'm dying to know more. Dick says the experts at the Mayo handle lots of patients every year; he assured me that Shirley's in good hands and in general good health. I may even get to see her tomorrow."

"That's great, Jeni. Now, what can I do to cheer you up tonight? Take you to dinner? Take you in my arms?"

"Hmmm," Jennifer exhaled, relaxing her shoulders, and melting into her husband's embrace as he gently removed the empty wine glass from her fingers.

Fourteen

THE following day, Jennifer went about completing routine household chores, keeping her phone in a side pocket. She checked it from time to time to be sure the ringer was on, looking for a missed text or call. Finally, at eleven o'clock, she felt its vibration and heard the special chime she had programmed in for Dick Harrington.

"I have news," he said when she answered. "Our girl is going into Phoenix to the Cocci Clinic. It's a part of the Mayo system, a comprehensive testing facility, the best in the country. From there, she'll go to the hospital down the street, at least for another day or two, while we wait for results. I'm not sure what happens after that. So that's the bad news, I guess. The good news is that she requested to see you, and we wondered if you would be able to come for a short visit tomorrow afternoon, around four?"

"This is sounding very serious, Dick. And of course I'll come. Is there anything you would like me to bring?"

"Just your sweet self. It's a big campus, but the signage is good. Come to the main hospital entrance; there's plenty of visitor parking. Hours are eight to eight, but four tends to be a good time in the ebb and flow of hospital life. The reception desk can give you Shirley's room number and point you to the elevators. No flowers or other plant material allowed in the room."

"Got it. And thank you for calling. Please give Shirley my love. I'll see you at four tomorrow." *Is it my imagination, Dick, or did you just gloss over my concern? What are you not telling me?*

Jennifer dusted and scrubbed until the condo sparkled. She found housework satisfying, and rarely engaged a cleaner. But she always ended up in the kitchen, and today, after putting away her cleaning supplies, she set about making two of her favorite treats: gingerbread cookies, and currant butter scones.

As she baked, she reflected on the weekend trip she and John had taken recently with their friends. The four were in the car together for at least five hours. They had shared cocktails and meals and nightcaps two days in a row, and yet neither of the Harringtons had uttered a word about the heartbreak of their earlier years. If they had, she thought, she could have empathized with them. It would be something she and Shirley had in common, not that her disappointment in being childless, and her friend's grief over losing a beloved child, were the same thing. But still…

The next day, Jennifer prepared for her hospital visit by assembling a small gift package—some special tea packets, a few of the cookies and scones, and a delicate china teacup from the small collection she had purchased at various antique shops over the years. She arranged these items in a basket lined with a floral-patterned napkin, then stood back to admire the effect. *Charming.*

After changing her clothes and brushing her hair and teeth, she texted John, letting him know she was heading out, suggesting perhaps they meet somewhere in Scottsdale or Fountain Hills for dinner. She had put the address of the Mayo Clinic Hospital into her phone: thirty-eight minutes from Tonto Verde if she took Rio Verde Drive to Pima, forty-four if she went through Fountain Hills. Phoenix traffic never let up; she chose the faster route and added a cushion for road construction or fender-benders.

As it turned out, there were no incidents to slow her down, and she made every green light. Arriving at the hospital at ten minutes after four, she found a parking place under a tree that provided a little respite from the sun and pulled the folding aluminum shade across the dash. With the gift basket in her hands, she clicked the lock with her fob, and headed toward the entrance.

The reception area featured comfortable chairs arranged in intimate groupings, with current editions of popular magazines on side tables. Jennifer chose a corner chair and sat down to wait, killing time by checking her phone for messages and scrolling through news headlines. Finally, she approached the reception desk, where a woman whose badge indicated she was a volunteer looked up from the book she was reading, smiling at Jennifer's request and consulting a list of patients before pointing her in the direction of a bank of elevators.

Shirley's room, number seven hundred, was immediately to the right as Jennifer exited the elevator. The door stood partially open, and her friend was raised to a half-sitting position in her hospital bed. The light was dim, and it appeared to Jennifer she was sleeping. When she entered the room, however, Shirley opened her eyes, and a smile of recognition brightened her face.

"Jennifer, come in, how nice to see you. Come sit here in this chair next to the bed. What I have isn't contagious; I'm sure Dick told you. He's here in the building, taking a very late lunch with some former colleagues. Thank you so much for coming."

"I missed being with you on Tuesday," said Jennifer, "and I've been worried about you. I brought you some treats, and some tea. I hope these are things you can have."

"Thank you, dear. You're very thoughtful. I can eat and drink whatever I can keep down, and today that's anything I've been given." She peeked into the basket Jennifer placed beside her, crooning over its contents, then asked abruptly, "Have I ever told you that I lost a child?"

Jennifer gave a little gasp. "No, you haven't. But I know about it, from one of the Lady Putters. She told me your son died when he was just a young man. I'm so sorry, and I'd like to know more, if it isn't too painful to talk about."

"It was, for many years. But lately, I find myself wanting to talk about Richie, wanting to bring his memory back to life."

"Please tell me more," encouraged Jennifer. This was the opening she had been waiting for, that she had been afraid might never come.

"Dick and I postponed having children because of his studies—medical school is a long slog, pardon my slang. We thought he would finish school and complete his residency and then we would start our family—two, three, even four little ones. But when the time came, I couldn't get pregnant. I began to dread my time of the month, experienced it as a personal failure. Dick, of course, was always supportive. He never said a discouraging word. But people who didn't know us well would ask if we had children, or if we planned to have them. I dreaded those questions, so much so that I declined social invitations, even stepped away from the church for a while, though our friends there were so kind."

She paused. Jennifer waited; she was all too familiar with those questions.

"In vitro fertilization was new but was being offered at the Mayo Clinic in Rochester, which is where Dick had finally landed. He took me out to dinner one night and asked me if I'd like to try it. It's expensive, and insurance doesn't always pay, but our plan, which was through the clinic, did. And of course, it doesn't always work. But it worked for me, on the first try. We were elated."

At that point Dick walked into the room. "Hello, dear," said Shirley. "How was your lunch?"

Dick bent to kiss his wife on the cheek, then did the same to Jennifer. He pulled a chair around to the other side of Shirley's bed and sat down. "Lunch was fine", he replied, "but not as good as the chicken casserole I ate last night. Tonight, I plan to attack the lasagna."

Shirley smiled. "I hope I'll be home before you eat it all; lasagna's my favorite."

Dick nodded encouragement. "I'm eager to take you home, darling. How are you feeling?"

"Better, now that Jennifer's here, although I admit talking fatigues me. I was telling her about our son. I've been wanting her to know."

At those words Jennifer rose. If Shirley's disclosure had surprised her husband, Jennifer wasn't picking up on it. But she didn't want to tire her friend.

"I'm looking forward to hearing more about Richie, and perhaps seeing some pictures when you're back home. And don't worry, if Dick eats all the lasagna, I'll make more; it's John's favorite too. I'm leaving the two of you alone now; hopefully you can get a little nap." She squeezed Shirley's hand, smiled at Dick, and left the room.

Fifteen

LATER, sitting on barstools at Sapori d'Italia in Fountain Hills, where "happy hour from four o'clock to close" was the tag line, Jennifer filled John in on her visit with Shirley and the revelation about the Harringtons' son, a fact she hadn't wanted to share until she heard it firsthand. Still, she was spare with the details; they seemed fragile, like a tiny bird that had fallen from its nest.

When she'd finished, John gave her an account of *his* day, a productive one apparently, involving a meeting with a group of orthopedic surgeons.

"It's a big practice, twenty docs, twelve men and eight women, all brilliant, but nice, not full of themselves. I'd say their ages range from thirty-five to sixty-five. They're concerned about practice continuation—what happens when one or more of them retires, or, God forbid, one of them becomes disabled or dies. They need to be prepared to buy that partner's shares. And of course, each partner wants his share of the practice protected for his family; I mean, these guys and gals make a ton of money."

"I know you've explained this to me before, but it's a little confusing."

"It seems that way, but it's simple, really—a classic business problem—whether it's doctors, or lawyers, or architects. The group's attorney drafts an agreement that lays out the formula for valuing their shares, and clarifies trigger points that would cause them to be bought or sold. My job is to make sure they can come up with the money when it's needed.

"They seemed to genuinely appreciate my ideas, gave me the green light to proceed in putting together proposals for their practice manager's review. Greg Thornburg's his name. I met him through their accounting firm, played a round of golf with the managing partner recently, one of the leads McDougal provided. Things are happening, Jeni."

He raised his glass to hers. She toasted him, then asked, "But how *do* they come up with the money?"

He smiled. "Life insurance. Big policies on each of them, front-end loaded, with cash values that can be used to fund a deferred compensation plan if they aren't needed for the buyout. The real coup was being able to meet with all the docs at their quarterly meeting, not one of them absent. That's rare, speaks to the respect they have for each other. We'll satisfy their professional needs, then hopefully I'll meet with each one of them individually to evaluate their personal needs. This case could go on for months, Jeni, but it'll be worth it." This was John at his best, she thought—upbeat, excited.

They finished their wine, and the order of fried ravioli they had shared from the happy hour menu, as the chicken parmigiana and Caesar salad they planned to take home to enjoy on their own patio was delivered with the check. They left the restaurant in their separate cars, driving across town and through the desert park as the sun disappeared on the horizon, its afterglow illuminating the distinctive four peaks.

Sixteen

SHIRLEY Harrington slept through the teatime she had anticipated, and now sat up in bed with her dinner tray, watching the evening news with her husband. She had encouraged him to leave the hospital for home after Jennifer left, suggesting he meet up with his friends at the grill for a beer, or enjoy a swim. But Dick had elected to stay, listening to her breathing, watching a muted Diamondbacks game, and occasionally dozing off in his chair.

She offered to share her meal, but he reminded her he had lasagna in the refrigerator, and both agreed there was no contest. When the PBS News Hour concluded, he turned off the television and gave her an affectionate look.

"Did you enjoy your visit with Jennifer?" he asked.

"Very much," she responded. "She's like a younger sister, or even a daughter. It's strange, I have so many friends, but Jennifer is more than a friend. I told her about my struggle to have children, and then about finally getting pregnant, and it felt good to share those confidences with another woman, after so many years. You know I always say, 'God is full of surprises', and Jennifer has been one of those unexpected blessings for me."

"I agree, she's a lovely person," said Dick. "And I like John, too. From what I can gather, things are going quite well for him with his new firm. When you're back home and totally recovered, we'll have them over for dinner and reciprocate. I'll probe a little to see if there are any doors I can help open for John in the medical community."

At that, he stood and kissed her gently on the cheek, wishing her a good night's sleep as he left the room. She'd just closed her eyes again when she heard him say "good night" at the nearby nurses' station.

Seventeen

THE Fourth of July holiday in Fountain Hills was a big deal, as the man-made lake in the center of town offered one of the few venues in the desert where fireworks could safely be deployed. Partygoers came from all over the area to listen to live music and enjoy the array of food trucks that surrounded the perimeter, as they waited for the sun to set and the pyrotechnics to begin. Face-painting, balloons, ice cream cones and paletas delighted the children. The many booths displaying arts and crafts extended the length of the grassy median from La Montana to Fountain Hills Boulevard, and the bars that lined Palisades Boulevard on either side of the median, with their outdoor patios and misters, teemed with revelers.

Frank Chavez and his family were among the crowd. He was on active duty along with several other deputies, patrolling the area on foot to meet and greet the citizens and to assure the celebration didn't get out of hand. Margaret and his mother had set the table they'd arrived early to reserve with a checkered cloth and a red plastic beer cup filled with daisies and small American flags. Fried chicken, potato salad, and brownies were nestled among ice packs in the cooler, and warm pork green chili tamales were packed in a colorful Mexican basket, their wafting fragrance making it hard to resist early sampling. Scottie and Ginny had set out on their scooters to circle the lake and look for friends they hadn't seen since school let out a month earlier.

He'd given the kids a seven o'clock dinner time, which should give his sister, Maria, time to finish her shift at the clinic in Scottsdale as well as stop by her apartment to change before joining them in the park. She had phoned earlier to say she planned to bring a friend from work, assuming there was enough food.

He took one more loop around the grounds, reminding several people their dogs absolutely must be on leash—no exceptions!—and helping a young boy and his sister locate their mother, who was only a few feet away from them, but obstructed from view by the crowds. He rejoined his family just as his sister and another woman walked up.

Frank hugged Maria. "Frank Chavez," he said, offering his big hand to her friend.

"June Lambreth," responded the dark-haired beauty, placing a creamy, manicured hand in his. "Y'all are so sweet to include me in your family picnic. I hope you like pecan tassies." She placed the plastic-covered paper plate she held in her left hand on the table.

Frank smiled broadly. "I've never tasted one, but they look delicious. I'm guessing from your accent that this is a southern delicacy."

June smiled. "It was one of my family's favorite recipes when I was growing up in Charlotte."

Introductions were made all around, and cups of iced lemonade were poured. When the six family members and their guest were seated at the table with the food spread out on it, everyone beamed their thanks and praise for the cooks. It was one of Frank's favorite meals and he savored every bite.

"So, here's what's happening at the clinic," said Maria, with a nod to her colleague. "This is shaping up to be a bad year for Valley fever. A prominent doc brought his wife in with it several weeks ago. We had her overnight, then they moved her to Phoenix. I hear she's been in and out of the hospital ever since."

"What kind of fever?" the twins asked. They often spoke in unison, a twin thing that never failed to make Frank smile.

"Valley fever—I'd never heard of it either!" said June.

"It happens every year in the Southwest, northern Mexico too, but this year our cases are more severe," Maria explained to her nieces. "But you don't need to worry," she reassured them.

The conversation turned to the summer heat, the girls' plans to begin soccer practice, and the price of eggs at the supermarket. As he often did, Frank basked in the glow of "his girls", as he collectively referred to the five females in his family. Finally, he pulled his six-foot frame up from the table to make another round of the park, which was buzzing with excitement as a few preliminary rockets were released against the darkening sky.

Eighteen

THE sixth of July was a Wednesday, and despite the heat Jennifer had signed up to putt. She was looking to take her mind off Shirley, who was back in the hospital. She secretly hoped Dick would text her an invitation to visit her friend, in which case she would cancel her putting reservation. In fact, as she came off the course and headed toward lunch in the clubhouse, she saw that she had a voice mail message from him, saying that Shirley would be released the following day and suggesting that Jennifer come over on Friday, assuming Shirley slept well Thursday night.

"If there's one thing that's hard to do in the hospital," he said, "it's to get a good night's sleep. Shirley's looking forward to being in her own bed tomorrow night."

Friday morning, Jennifer rang the Harringtons' doorbell at ten-thirty, and entered their spacious living room, where Shirley sat almost upright in Dick's recliner.

"How are you today?" Jennifer asked, thinking her friend seemed smaller, and more tired and pale than ever. The last month had been difficult, with short intermittent visits to her friend between home and hospital, during which Shirley mostly slept. Jennifer had brought meals faithfully to the house, and Dick, who seemed older and more haggard himself as the weeks wore on, claimed to rely on them.

Today he brought coffee to the women, fumbling the tray as he set it down and spilling the hot liquid into their saucers. "I'm sorry," he said, smiling ruefully, heading back to the kitchen and returning with a paper towel.

"I feel fine," Shirley said, "although, every time I think I'm better, it seems I have a relapse. These hospital stays are starting to run together in my mind. As nice as the nurses are, I don't really want to know them all by name." She gave a little laugh.

Jennifer nodded sympathetically and took a sip of her coffee.

"Do you mind if we talk about Richie?" Shirley sat a little taller in her chair.

"Of course not—I've been so wanting to hear more." Shirley had told Jennifer during one of their visits how ecstatic she and Dick had been about her pregnancy, how she had reveled in her morning sickness, eating soda crackers and drinking peppermint tea, loving her baby bump and splurging on maternity clothes.

"Where did I leave off? Everything seemed to be going fine, until a routine ultrasound raised a red flag—a possible congenital heart defect. It's the most common fetal abnormality, but of course, no one expects it to happen to *their* baby. We were afraid, but calm."

Shirley became more animated. Jennifer listened with rapt attention.

"My doctors—now I had a team of them—instructed us to have a fetal echocardiogram at twenty weeks. It revealed what the doctors agreed was an atrioventricular septal defect, one of the more common congenital heart defects, and one that can be more, or less, serious. We had to wait and see, and I will tell you, Jennifer, it is the most agonizing kind of waiting a woman can endure.

"Many women who know their babies are being born with CHDs—that my dear, is the acronym for Congenital Heart Defect— choose birth by Cesarean section. But I didn't want the recovery time involved after that surgery, especially given the other unknowns, and my doctors allowed me to choose a normal delivery, with the C-section as a backup should my labor not go well. Just after midnight on his due date, our baby boy began to announce his impending birth, and Dick and I headed to the hospital, which was only a few blocks away. My water had broken, and my labor pains gradually intensified, all according to divine plan. I welcomed each contraction, praying for the next. I wanted our child on the outside, where I could hold him and examine him."

Shirley stopped to drink her coffee, which at this point had cooled. Jennifer wanted to offer to heat it but didn't dare interrupt.

"Richard Rutherford Harrington, named for his father and my family, was born at six o'clock in the morning, seven pounds and two ounces, and visibly perfect in every way. I did what most new mothers do, counted his fingers and toes and gently touched his amazingly soft skin, before the team of pediatric cardiologists whisked him away from the room and another team of obstetricians and nurses began to repair the slight tears I incurred during the delivery."

She paused again, and this time Jennifer did offer to refresh her coffee, an offer Shirley accepted. The older woman sipped from her cup and took a small bite of the biscuit Jennifer had placed on her saucer. Then she continued.

"Of course, Richie's problem was invisible, and it was life-threatening. But it was treatable, with cause for hope for—if not a normal life, a full life—though one with a shortened expectancy.

There were surgeries, weeks spent in the neonatal intensive care unit connected to tubes and wires, and doctors and nurses who, like angels, administered to Richie's every need. At times, I could hold him, but more often I just sat by his hospital crib and stroked his flawless little face and the bottoms of his feet, as pink and soft as rose petals. I tried to nurse him, but it didn't work out, and my milk supply gradually dried up. Richie squeezed my finger with his tiny fist, like a normal infant, and when he smiled at me for the first time I almost wept, though that first smile was probably the result of gas," Shirley said, with a little laugh.

"Dick, of course, had his work. The clinic was extremely generous with his time off, but reality set in, and his shifts were sometimes twenty-four hours. By now he had made the decision to sub-specialize in pediatric cardiology. He was a sponge for knowledge that could benefit his own child and others with heart conditions.

"When we finally brought Richie home, at almost three months, we hired a nurse to come in at night so that I could sleep and keep my strength up during the day. The women of the church organized our meals for a few weeks, and we settled into a new life that gradually became our routine. Richie put on weight, and progressed according to the pediatrician's charts, and although he had more doctors' appointments than a typical infant, we had what seemed to us like a conventional life."

Whereas on other days talking had seemed to tire Shirley, today it seemed to energize her. Jennifer shifted her position on the sofa, leaning in.

"I had no siblings, and our parents and Dick's sister, who never married, did not live near us. Our Gloria Dei Lutheran Church community, which was just a few minutes' drive from our home, was our family. Richie had playmates in the nursery there, and he and a few of the boys and girls whose parents we were friends with, some of whom also worked at the clinic, became close over the years. These children knew about our son's condition, but they didn't treat him like he was different. They all attended school together, and this spirit of inclusion carried over there, so that Richie's social development seemed typical.

"As the kids got older, they became involved in sports. Richie was allowed to participate, as long as he followed his care team's protocols, which he did. His coaches were very understanding. I drew the line, however, at sleepaway camp. I couldn't bear the thought of him having a medical event miles away from me and Dick and the doctors who cared for him—away from the hospital we knew, which was like a lighthouse to me.

"This is why, when it came time to choose a college, I encouraged him to stay in town and attend our local branch of the state university. But he had his heart set on Macalester, which his guidance counselor described as a perfect fit, and which was less than two hours away. The icing on the cake was an academic scholarship. Richie had written his college essay about his experience living with a congenital heart defect, and it impressed the admissions committee. Dick and I helped our son move into his dorm room in August of 1999, then drove home to Rochester, Dick consoling me as I wept, assuring me that everything would be fine."

Jennifer nodded sympathetically.

"We tried not to hover. I took up quilting, not my thing in hindsight, but it helped take my mind off missing my son, even as I lovingly stitched together squares of MAC blue and orange, black and white, and two shades of gray, the Macalester palette. This hand tied coverlet was my Christmas gift to our son when he returned home after his first semester away. That holiday break was a joyous time for our little family of three. We baked traditional Swedish cookies and pastries, decorated the tree, and held an open house for our close friends and their families."

Jennifer imagined this happy time, so different from her own family holiday memories.

"The young people had all chosen colleges around the country, and it was a parent's delight to see them reunited and hear them share stories of their time apart. There was a girl Richie had been friends with since they were toddlers. Her name was Celeste. She had clear blue eyes that seemed to laugh, which she did often, and she wore her blond hair in a pixie cut, different from most of the others her age, with their long ponytails. The church youth group had always done things in a crowd, even attending their senior prom as a group. But over that Christmas break Richie and Celeste singled each other out, and by the time he headed back to St. Paul and she to Fort Worth, where she attended Texas Christian University, they were a couple. Everything seemed so perfect, the school he had chosen, a girlfriend…" Her voice trailed off, and she leaned back in her chair, eyes closed.

"Shirley," Jennifer rose, "this must be exhausting for you. Please take some time alone now. I can come back tomorrow, or even later today. I'm eager to hear as much as you feel like sharing with me."

"That's very thoughtful of you, dear," the older woman responded with half-closed lids. "I want you to know my son; he would only be a few years younger than you. But you're right, I should rest. I need to get my strength back. I don't mean to sound dramatic, but this illness has forced me to face my own mortality. Losing a child is something you never get over, but Dick and I have had each other to lean on. I'm not sure how he would cope without me."

"Well let's not go there," said Jennifer. "I'm here when you feel like talking more, so please call me. And when you do regain your strength, we can get back to our Tuesday routine. Everyone will be so happy to see you. You rest now—I'll let myself out." She patted her friend on the arm, then exited through the magnificent, carved front doors.

Nineteen

SHIRLEY Harrington lay back in her chair and let herself drift into a shallow sleep. When she opened her eyes, her husband was sitting where Jennifer had sat, quietly turning the pages of a medical periodical. He smiled tenderly at her. "May I serve you a little lunch? Jennifer's tuna salad?"

"That and a few crackers would be nice," she responded. "And a glass of iced tea, please."

When they had their plates and had begun to eat, Shirley told her husband again how close she felt to her younger friend. "I feel as though she could be a little sister, or perhaps my own child. Since I never had a sister or a daughter, I can only imagine what those bonds are like. I find myself wanting to spend time with Jennifer in a way I don't remember feeling about anyone else, except for you, of course, and Richie. But I've been monopolizing the conversation. There's so much I'd like to know about her—her earlier life, her parents. She never mentions them. And I wonder why she and John don't have children." She paused to take a bite.

"It sounds as though the two of you have a lot to talk about," Dick offered.

Twenty

THE following morning Jennifer received a call from Dick. Shirley had not had a great night's sleep but would still like to see her if she could stop by. Jennifer decided to walk the mile to the Harrington home, even though the thermostat registered ninety degrees.

"I've done all the talking lately," Shirley said, adjusting her small body in the recliner, as Jennifer settled into her regular sofa seat. "Let's talk about you. What were your parents like, and how did you and John meet?"

Jennifer told Shirley about growing up in a home where she often felt alone, where she was, in fact, often alone. She confessed that she longed to be friends with the other girls but felt embarrassed to invite them to the rundown houses and cheap apartments her family lived in, so she never accepted the invitations to their birthday parties and sleepovers.

Shirley nodded sympathetically.

"I never even dated, until I met John," Jennifer said, and smiled as she told Shirley about their courtship and marriage.

Shirley then broached her next question.

"If you don't mind my asking, Jennifer, why did you and John choose not to have children, or was it a choice?"

Jennifer hesitated. She wanted to answer Shirley honestly, and she wanted to remain loyal to John.

"As you've gathered," she waded in, "I didn't have the happiest childhood, and there weren't really any children in my life—no siblings or cousins, no babysitting gigs. I didn't have confidence around children, and certainly not around babies. John and I had a very romantic relationship—we still do, actually—but in the early days it was electric, and we didn't make much space for anyone else in our orbit.

"However, when it came time to either choose to have children or remain childless forever, we decided to go for it. We were so much in love, and we became excited about the idea of sharing our lives with a little human being that we created. I had turned thirty-five, so we weren't sure how long it would take me to become pregnant, or if I even could. But we enjoyed trying." Jennifer laughed self-consciously. Shirley smiled.

"Then, the Great Recession happened. It was hard for everyone, of course, but devastating for us. John's income went from a healthy six figures to almost nothing, even though he still worked twenty-four, seven. At one point we thought we might lose our house; we struggled to make the payments, and its value had dropped below what we paid for it, so we wondered, 'what's the point?'. I had a parttime job that didn't pay much to begin with, so was among the first to be let go..."

"I'm so sorry," murmured Shirley. "It must have been difficult."

"It was," agreed Jennifer, "but the worst was still to come."

Shirley raised her eyebrows.

"John counseled his clients to stay the course, to ride out the market and hold on to their investments. But he didn't follow his own advice. Our portfolio values dropped so low that in March of 2009, he couldn't take it any longer. He sold everything we had, at what turned out to be the bottom, or close to it. Of course, the market recovered, and his clients have done great; he didn't lose a one of them. But *we* have spent the past thirteen years trying to get back to where we were, or rather, where we would have been."

As she spoke these words, she felt overwhelmed—sad, angry, or afraid—she wasn't sure.

"So there you have it. There are thousands of stories like ours; trillions of dollars in net worth were lost in those years. It's just that, you know, John is a professional, and feels he should have known better. So it still haunts him.

"But to answer the question you asked me, Shirley, we were so under water at that point we decided we couldn't afford a child." *That, and the fact that for almost a year John suffered from a depression so severe that we rarely made love.*

"I'm so sorry," Shirley repeated. "You would have been a wonderful mother, a natural."

"Thank you, and thank you for taking me under your wing. I'm beginning to feel I belong here. When you're back on your feet, I'd like to host a dinner party to celebrate. I'm not sure about my ability to pull it off in our small space, but I'd like to try. Our home in Santa Monica was lovely—also small, but with a charming patio, perfect for entertaining. Fortunately, the market was strong when we sold it to move here last year, and we were able to invest some of the proceeds, so we're getting there!"

Normally Jennifer cared far too much what other people thought of her for this much self-disclosure, but Shirley's genuine interest and her obvious concern made it easy to allow herself to be vulnerable.

When she left shortly thereafter the two women hugged each other goodbye.

Twenty-one

THE following week, while the rest of their foursome putted out at the eighteenth green, Dick Harrington took John aside and asked if they could arrange a private meeting in John's office one day soon. "I'd like to discuss a personal matter," he said. John checked the schedule on his watch. "Tomorrow morning?" he suggested, making a mental note to reserve a conference room.

He started to tell Jennifer about the appointment that night, but for some reason declined to do so. He rarely kept anything from her, but he respected his clients' confidentiality, and this situation, though he had no idea what it was, might call for discretion.

Dick arrived promptly at the appointed time, and John led him to a conference room that was small but adequate. They both accepted a glass of water from one of the office assistants. Dick walked to the window to admire the view.

When both men were seated, they engaged in a few minutes of small talk, with Dick asking how the relocation of his practice was going and John able to say honestly that things couldn't be better. Dick then pulled a plastic sleeve from his cloth satchel-style briefcase and removed the life insurance policy it held.

"I'd like your help in changing the beneficiary on this," he said.

"Of course," John responded, "that's a routine procedure for the back office. If we don't have your company's paperwork we can use a universal form. Are you and Shirley in the process of updating your estate plans?"

"In a way, yes, although this is the only change we have in mind for now. It's a second-to-die policy, purchased in the early eighties, when even a modest estate was subject to federal transfer taxes. We had a son, Richie. He died in 2000. I'm sure Jennifer must have shared some of the details with you."

"She has, Dick, and we're both so sorry for your loss. There really aren't words…"

"It's been over twenty years," Dick nodded, "but it's a life sentence. We originally bought this policy to protect our assets for Richie. It was owned by a life insurance trust, with a special needs trust receiving any proceeds not needed for taxes and settlement costs.

"When Richie died, given changes to the tax tables and our own situation, we decided to roll the policy out of the trust, pay the penalty, and resume ownership of it ourselves, give ourselves more flexibility. We made the Mayo Foundation the beneficiary. The clinic has done so much for us, and the staff is like family. Fact is, we made the foundation the primary beneficiary of our entire estate. Our parents didn't need the money, and have since passed, and my sister never married and did quite well for herself. She's also gone at this point. We haven't really had anyone else to think about after our deaths."

"So, what change are you looking to make?" asked John.

"We'd like your wife to receive half the proceeds of the policy, with the foundation receiving the other half."

John fumbled the pen he was holding, then recovered it. "Jennifer?" he asked. "But why?"

"She's been a godsend, John. Shirley is so fond of her, thinks of her as the daughter she never had. She says that often. This recent bout with Valley fever was a close call for her; she thought she was dying. I can tell you honestly, John, since she isn't here, that I did too, and I didn't know what I would do without her. She's had a bad case of it, and at her age even a mild case is serious. She isn't out of the woods yet; she's still terribly weak.

"We're blessed with friends, and they've all been supportive. But Jennifer has been a lifeline, nurturing our bodies with the delicious food she brings, and nurturing Shirley emotionally in the way only another woman can. Would you believe, that in all the years we've been in Arizona, there isn't a soul she has confided in about the loss of our son? Everyone knows, of course. But talking about it to Jennifer has been cathartic for Shirley. It's brought her peace."

John nodded.

"Anyway, Shirley raised the issue of the life insurance policy, and I agreed with her." He paused, adding, "The foundation will still be receiving a generous donation."

"What *is* the face amount of the policy, Dick?"

"Two million."

This time John managed to maintain his grip on the pen, as myriad questions flooded his brain: Conflict of interest? Undue influence? Best practices? He couldn't help but wonder if one or both Harringtons lacked mental capacity.

As if reading his mind, Dick answered, "I can assure you, John, that Shirley and I are both mentally sound, and we arrived at this decision together. Jennifer doesn't know anything about it, but of course I won't ask you to keep it from her. Remember, this policy doesn't pay off until we're both gone, and for an eighty-two-year-old man, I'm in excellent health. We could both live to be a hundred, you know."

John tamped down his thoughts and resumed his professional advisory role. "Thank you for your confidence in me, Dick, and thank you for your generosity to Jennifer. I'm happy to help you and Shirley carry out your wishes. If you're sure this change is what you want, I can have the paperwork prepared for your signatures.

"You'll need a witness, and I will recuse myself because of my relationship to the beneficiary. Although it can be anyone, it might be good if you asked one of your professional advisors—your attorney, perhaps—to witness your signatures. The forms can be ready for you in a day or so, and I'm happy to bring them to your home. Shirley doesn't need to come here.

"Would you mind leaving the policy with me? I'll give you a receipt for it."

The two men stood to shake hands. John walked Dick back to the reception area, then carried the policy to his office for safekeeping in a locked fireproof drawer. For a long while he sat at his desk, staring out the window at the sleek jets taking off and landing, imagining what a million tax-free dollars could do for him and his wife.

PART TWO

Twenty-two

THE crawl back to Tonto Verde in rush hour traffic was slow going, but John was in no hurry, and barely noticed the occasional overheated or disabled vehicle on the roadside that slowed things down even more. Many days, he called Jennifer to give her his ETA, but today he was too preoccupied. When he pulled into the driveway and pushed the remote opener, he was alarmed to find he didn't remember a thing about the drive home.

Jennifer greeted him at the garage door with a peck on the cheek. "How was your day?"

"Would you make me a drink, Jeni? A strong one, please. I'll change and be right with you."

"Sure thing, hon."

He recognized the look of concern on her face as she removed the bottles of gin and vermouth from the bar cart to the kitchen counter, where he heard the unmistakable sound of ice cubes hitting the metal shaker. He headed for their bedroom, closing the door behind him.

Ten minutes later, when he emerged and entered the kitchen, his wife added the liquor to the ice and shook them vigorously before pouring his martini into a chilled glass. "Olive or twist?" He waved his hand to indicate neither. She poured herself a glass of white wine from an open bottle in the refrigerator and joined him on the sofa.

"Give it up," she coaxed.

He dove in. "I had a visit from Dick today, at the office. He'd asked me for a meeting after our round yesterday. He'd said it was personal. I thought he probably wanted to help me with some introductions at the clinic. But this was about him and Shirley. He brought a life insurance policy with him, a policy that pays two million dollars after they both die. He asked me to help change the beneficiary on it, so that one million dollars would go to you." He waited to get her reaction before continuing.

"To me?" she asked, her eyes wide. "But why?"

"Dick says Shirley really wants this, that she thinks of you as a daughter, that they have no family, and that the Mayo, which is the other beneficiary, still inherits the bulk of their property. They're very grateful for the care you've shown them, Jeni, during Shirley's illness. And I agree with him, you've been wonderful. But a million dollars?" He shook his head.

"I told Dick I could help, but that having their attorney sign as witness to the change would be good. I guess I'm thinking the attorney might try to talk them out of it, or at least be sure they've thought it through. Honestly, I was baffled.

"But then, after he left, I couldn't keep myself from dreaming a little. I wasn't sure if I should tell you; but then, how could I not? I don't want this to affect your relationship—our relationship—with the Harringtons."

"Does Dick think Shirley's dying?"

"He said she's not out of the woods yet—those were his words. This policy pays at the second of both their deaths, so even if Shirley died now, the policy would not pay out. Please don't cry, Jeni. I don't think she's dying. I'm just explaining to you how this kind of thing works." He put his arm around her and pulled her close, caressing her hair.

He felt her relax, and he released her, sinking back into the sofa and retreating into the privacy of his thoughts. He watched as the sun disappeared below the horizon, and the bats began their nightly flight, darting below the patio eaves for nocturnal insects before returning to their crevices in the rocky desert mountains. He heard the coyotes in the park, their yips and howls momentarily drowned out by a lone jet flying over toward Sky Harbor.

Twenty-three

THE following morning John left early. "A breakfast meeting in Paradise Valley," he explained to Jennifer, "very important, wish me luck."

"You'll do great!" she assured him with a kiss.

Neither said a word about the previous night's conversation. Jennifer had questions she didn't know how to articulate. By default, she proceeded with her day as though nothing had happened, enjoying a second cup of coffee, and tidying the condo as the spicy aroma of a fresh apple cake wafted through the unit. When the timer went off, she tested it with a toothpick, and, satisfied it was done, removed it from the oven to a rack on the countertop.

She still had time for a walk to the fitness center in the clubhouse for a quick workout before she planned to visit Shirley, and according to the bathroom scale, onto which she had stepped with trepidation, she needed both the walk and the workout. Normally she exercised at least three times a week, but recently her routine had gotten off track. "You need to get back into shape," she had chided her reflection in the mirror.

Showering later, she felt invigorated, and she made a mental vow to practice better self-care, no matter what. She tied the straps of a blue and white checked seersucker sundress behind her neck and slipped into flat sandals, pulling her hair into a high ponytail and spritzing a bit of cologne behind her ears. Her cheeks were still pink from the exercise. A flick of mascara, and a touch of lip gloss, and she was ready to walk out the door.

Today, she decided to take their recently purchased used golf cart to the Harringtons'. She placed half of the cake on the floor for the short ride.

Dick greeted her at the door, giving Jennifer a light kiss on the cheek and taking the foil-covered plate from her. He led her into the living room, where Shirley sat in the recliner, her breathing audible.

"How are you today, dear?" She spoke slowly.

"I'm fine, Shirley, how are you?" Jennifer leaned down and wrapped her arms around the bony shoulders, giving them a gentle hug.

"I'm tired, but not too tired for a visit with you. Thank you for coming." She offered a wan smile.

Jennifer sat next to her friend's chair. "I want to be here. I just wish you could knock this bug, or whatever it's called.

"And I as well. How is that handsome husband of yours?"

Jennifer smiled. "Well, he's still handsome, that's for sure. He had an important meeting today. He works hard, and he tells me things are going well."

"We're both blessed, aren't we, to have such wonderful men in our lives?" As if on cue, Dick appeared, carrying a tray with two cups of coffee and slices of the coffee cake. His visible tremor made the cups run over into their saucers.

"Let me help you with that, Dick," Jennifer stabilized the tray and guided it to rest on the table in front of her.

He smiled gratefully. "You girls try not to gossip too much," he said with a wink as he left the room.

After taking a bite of the cake and licking a tiny crumb from her finger, Shirley spoke. "Do you mind if I speak of Richie again? I haven't told you how he died."

"It was his heart condition," Jennifer said. "Wasn't it?"

"No, it wasn't. We were always prepared for that, but it isn't what happened. Richie died in an automobile accident. He and a friend were coming home for spring break, in March of his freshman year. Celeste was going to be in town, too. It had been such a good year for him, professors he liked, friends, a girlfriend…" Shirley smiled. "He was so excited to see her again. They had been writing and calling each other since Christmas.

"There was a storm, and the roads were treacherous. He shouldn't have come—should have waited. He was a good driver, but it wasn't safe. The car ahead of him lost control, and when the driver braked, Richie braked too. He was hit by the car behind him, slammed into the one in front, sandwiched between the two. Thank goodness his friend survived. He told us about the last few seconds of our son's life. It was no one's fault, and Richie was the only fatality. Everyone involved was so kind, so sorry for what happened. The patrolman who came to our home to tell us was fighting back tears. Dick and I just looked at each other and held each other tight. But we didn't cry, not then. We donated all his organs, except for his heart, of course. I like to think of that, someone living on with Richie's beautiful blue eyes."

Jennifer thought she might faint, and realized she was holding her breath. "Oh, Shirley," she said, exhaling. "I am so, so sorry. After all you had been through, all Richie had been through…to die like that. So young, so tragic. I am so, so sorry."

At this point Shirley leaned back in her chair and closed her eyes. Her breathing deepened, and Jennifer knew she was sleeping. She covered her friend's small hands with her own, squeezing them gently. Then she rose and carried the tray to the kitchen, setting it down carefully to avoid rattling the cups. She wrote a short note on a pad she found next to the phone and placed it near the tray. *I'm leaving now so that Shirley can rest. Please call if you need anything.* She made it out the door and all the way to the golf cart before she broke down in tears.

Twenty-four

JENNIFER had missed the Lady Putters several weeks in a row. This Wednesday, however, Dick was taking Shirley to the clinic for a visit with one of her doctors. At John's encouragement, Jennifer signed up to putt and to attend the lunch afterward.

"I know how devoted you are to Shirley," he had chided, "but don't neglect your other friendships."

"What other friendships?" she'd said, with a hint of sarcasm, before admitting he was right. She *had* made other friends here, acquaintances really, and knew instinctively she must nurture these relationships if they were to grow. John's gentle prodding was for the sake of her own happiness. In fact, almost everything John did was for the sake of her happiness.

When she arrived at the registration table and read the roster, she saw that she was paired with Gretchen Yarborough, whom she liked and wanted to get closer to. Dick told her that Gretchen had also been attentive during Shirley's illness. But the Yarboroughs had a daughter and grandchildren in Idaho, and often left Tonto to visit them. Still, Jennifer thought, a former hospice nurse must know just how to support friends in the Harringtons' situation. She felt gratitude toward Gretchen, and at the same time, a twinge of envy.

"Hi Jennifer, I've missed seeing you. Where've you been? Actually, I know the answer to that question. Dick Harrington told Gary you've been a lifeline for Shirley during her illness, like a daughter to them both." She gave Jennifer a little hug. "But I'm glad you came out today."

"Yes, Dick's taking Shirley to the doctor this morning." She hoped she wasn't being indiscreet.

"The last time I visited them she seemed subdued, but as always, gracious. Such a lovely person. Such a sad life."

"Yes," Jennifer agreed, knowing her voice suggested a vague sense of longing. She cleared her throat. "Possibly the loveliest person I've ever known."

"Good morning! I think we're a threesome. I'm Nancy, Nancy Scott. I'm new."

"Hi Nancy, I'm Gretchen." Gretchen shook the hand that had been thrust in her direction. "Are you new to the Putters, or to Tonto Verde, or both?"

"Both! My husband and I recently bought a place on Montana Drive. We haven't sold our home in Denver yet, not sure if we will, we'll spend a summer here first and see. From what I understand, it's bearable if you stay inside with the AC on, but we're outdoors people. Are you here full-time? Ben's an architect, has his own firm, lots of mouths to feed, so he'll be back and forth. I'm a writer, working on a novel set in the desert. You must be Jennifer." She stopped talking long enough to take a breath, smiling broadly.

Jennifer responded in kind. She liked this woman—who seemed totally without pretense—immediately. Nancy had short, curly red hair, a smattering of freckles across her cheeks, and a slightly upturned nose. She wore no makeup. Jennifer thought she looked like a teenager, but judged her to be about her own age.

Nancy kept up a constant banter as they made their way around the course—unacceptable for regulation golf, Jennifer understood from John, but fine for this venue. The Lady Putters were there to socialize and make friends, and no one, with a few exceptions, took these games too seriously.

After golf, the threesome made their way to the clubhouse for lunch and more conversation. Jennifer realized she had not had this much fun or felt this light-hearted in months. Not, she realized, since her dear, older friend had become ill. She tried to push the thought of Shirley out of her mind, just for the next hour, but several women stopped by her table to ask how Shirley was doing, and soon she and Gretchen were telling Nancy about their mutual friend and her illness.

"Wow, Valley fever," said Nancy. "I've never heard of it, sounds awful. I hope she recovers soon. She's fortunate to have the two of you as friends. I can't wait to tell Ben I met you. Let's plan a happy hour—Shirley too, when she's better."

At that point the Putters' president attempted to quiet the high-pitched cacophony in the party room by pinging her water glass with a spoon. Reluctantly, the women lowered their voices and gradually stopped talking. A young man from the pro shop stepped forward to announce the day's winners, and to congratulate the few who had successfully holed their balls with one putt. He handed out envelopes with small bills, typically five or six dollars, to those on the teams with the lowest scores. A hole-in-one didn't result in a cash prize, but an accumulation of them earned a special pin, a highly coveted jewelry item in the Tonto Verde community.

Twenty-five

BY the time Jennifer bade Gretchen and Nancy goodbye, she was in high spirits, humming a Katy Perry tune as she walked the few blocks home. She was surprised to see John's car in the driveway, and to find him at his desk in the guest bedroom. Lately, he had gone into the Scottsdale office most days, explaining to her that being around his colleagues stimulated him and made him more productive. Jennifer never questioned John about his work schedule. His drive was one of the things she had always appreciated about him.

"I'm happy to see you home so early, but a little surprised. Did you decide to avoid the rush hour parking lot on the Pima Freeway?"

He rose to kiss her, then pulled her into a gentle embrace, nuzzling her hair and taking in the scent of her. "Let's sit down," he said, "and let me share some difficult news.

"Dick stopped by the office this morning to return the signed paperwork for the life insurance. He was in the area, so it was convenient for him. He had taken Shirley to the Cocci Clinic. He told me he was really concerned about her lack of improvement; she's very weak, and since last night she's been running a low-grade fever. Apparently, the doctors agreed; they re-admitted her to the hospital."

He stopped talking long enough to wipe a tear from her cheek with his thumb.

"Dick seemed discouraged," John continued, "and looked frail and tired himself. You know how news travels around this community, like wildfires in California. I decided to come home and tell you this myself. Don't cry, Jeni. Shirley's in the best place a person who is sick can be. The Mayo is preeminent."

"I need to go see her—did Dick say when I could come?"

"That's the other hard thing. Shirley's care team is limiting her visitors for the time being. Dick is allowed, of course, but no one else. It's temporary, baby," he said, holding her tight. "Just a precaution. When she's allowed to have visitors, you'll be the first one she wants to see."

Twenty-six

WHEN Dick Harrington rang Jennifer at nine o'clock that evening, Jennifer knew before answering what he would say.

"Our Shirley is gone. She died a few minutes ago, in her sleep. She looks peaceful. I think it was her time," he said, his voice calm, sounding almost relieved. "She's with Richie now."

"But I didn't get to tell her goodbye…" A cry of lament escaped her and brought John rushing from his office, where she knew he was preparing for an early meeting he had scheduled the next morning.

"What's wr–?" John fell silent as a look of comprehension spread across his face.

Jennifer nodded, too upset to speak. She drew him close to her, so that he could hear Dick's voice.

"Would you call Pastor Jean in the morning? Tell her I'll be in touch about a service. I'm going to stay here until they come for the…for her." Dick took a deep breath. "Then I think I'll get a few hours of rest before making the drive back to Tonto.

"Shirley told me again tonight, before she drifted off to sleep, that she loved you like a daughter, Jennifer. I hope you will take solace in knowing that."

Twenty-seven

JENNIFER called the church the next morning and got a recording indicating the pastor was in a meeting, or away from her desk. She left a vague message requesting a return call, then forced herself to make the bed and load the dishwasher, rewarding herself with a second cup of coffee for accomplishing these modest goals. John had offered to come back home after his meeting, but she had assured him she would be fine. She knew intellectually that a workout would ease the depression she felt. "Maybe later," she told herself.

When her phone rang, she assumed it was the call she was expecting, but to her surprise and delight it was Nancy. "Hey, Jennifer," enthused her new friend. "I'm driving into Fountain Hills for a meeting with the sheriff, just thought I'd check in with you and say 'hi'. I don't know how long I'll be in town, but depending on when I get back to Tonto, maybe we could have lunch, or take a walk, or both."

"I'm not sure what kind of company I'll be. My friend Shirley—the one Gretchen and I told you about who's been ill—passed away last night. I'm feeling pretty low, but I'd love to get together. Why don't you text me when you're headed toward home? I don't have anything on my calendar."

"You got it, girl. I'm really sorry about your friend. We'll…" Her voice cut out. Jennifer assumed Nancy had lost cell service as she drove into the desert park that separated the Verdes from the nearest town.

Her spirit lifted, Jennifer pulled on a pair of tights with a side pocket for her phone, located her earbuds, and headed for the fitness center. Only after she arrived there and was stretching out on the bars did she think to wonder why Nancy was meeting with the sheriff.

Twenty-eight

NANCY strode into the District Seven division of the Maricopa County Sheriff's Office and introduced herself to the receptionist. "I have a ten o'clock appointment with Deputy Chavez," she said, as a six-foot tall, uniformed man with a friendly smile exited an office at the end of the hall and strode toward her.

"Nancy Scott? I'm Frank Chavez," he extended his hand to her. "Welcome to the district. Can I make you a cup of coffee?" he offered. He led Nancy to his office and indicated two chairs at a round table in the corner.

She quickly surveyed the room. On one large wall, his University of Arizona diploma was surrounded by multiple awards and certificates. Four framed photographs, three of women, and one of two girls—a blond and a brunette—sat on his credenza. All but the older woman—his mother, she assumed—were smiling.

"No coffee for me, thank you." Nancy raised her water bottle. "I'm a one cup a day gal, usually consumed around five in the morning. Thank you so much for agreeing to see me!"

"Of course, any time. Did I understand you to say you're a writer?"

"I am," she said. "Mysteries. The series I'm currently working on is set in the desert, and one of my characters is the county sheriff. I've only recently moved to Arizona, and I'm looking for local color, the kind of information I can't get by just going online or reading the papers. By the way, my sheriff is a good guy, as I've heard you are. I wondered, and I know it's a big ask, if I might shadow you one day, observe the kind of things you routinely deal with. I promise not to get in the way, or to ask too many questions. I just want to get a feel for what a sheriff really does."

Frank laughed. "Of course, no problem. It can be, as you put it, routine. But it's never boring, at least not for me." He consulted the calendar on his phone and suggested the following Tuesday, explaining that Mondays involved staff meetings and reports.

"Perfect," Nancy said. "What time should I plan to be here?"

"Let's say nine o'clock. We'll make the rounds and then have lunch, maybe at Phil's, speaking of local color."

"I can't wait. Thank you so much! I'll let you get back to work now." Nancy rose and shook hands with the sheriff again. He accompanied her to the building exit and waved goodbye.

She made a quick stop at Basha's for a carton of milk and a bottle of wine, then headed for home, texting Jennifer as she started the car to suggest a short walk followed by lunch.

Twenty-nine

"**WE** can take Agua Verde to Tonto Verde, turn right, and walk to El Circulo Drive. Should I make a quick call to the hostess station and reserve a patio table under the misters? Thirty minutes, assuming neither of us succumbs to heatstroke before we get there."

"Please do," replied Nancy. "Mind if I use your powder room before we head out?"

"Of course not." Jennifer, who had showered and changed from her gym clothes to golf shorts and a sleeveless collared shirt, picked up her phone.

As the women left the house and found their stride, Jennifer asked, "And how is Sheriff Frank today?"

"You know him?"

"Not really, only by reputation. When I see him in his patrol car, I always give him a little wave, and he waves back. I've heard good things about him. May I ask why you were meeting with him?"

"Research."

"Research?" Jennifer echoed.

"For the mystery I'm working on. He agreed to let me ride with him next Tuesday—I can't wait! But, changing the subject, I'm very sorry about your friend's death. I don't think you were expecting this."

"No, I wasn't. If I had been…"

"Go on."

"If I had been, I would have told her how much she meant to me." Jennifer chose her words carefully. "I wasn't close to my own mother, and I didn't have any other female relatives or close family friends. If I were to create a role model for myself, a person to look up to and emulate, she would be like Shirley. I wish I had told her that. This may sound dramatic, because I hadn't known her that long, but I loved her. I already miss her so much."

"I'm very sorry," Nancy said, again. "And if it's any consolation, I imagine Shirley knew how much you cared for her. Feelings like that are hard to conceal."

"Thank you. It's reassuring to hear you say that."

They turned the corner, and Jennifer asked, "Is all your writing fiction? All mysteries?"

"Oh, I've written a little of everything, but with a name like Nancy, the genre is almost predestined. Growing up in the fifties, my mother was a big fan of the girl sleuth."

Jennifer smiled. She really did like this woman.

They arrived at the hostess station and gave their member numbers before being led to a table on the patio. Jennifer was pleasantly surprised by the number of women she could greet by name, thanks to Shirley, and Wednesday putting.

"Meet Nancy Scott—she and her husband moved to Tonto recently," she said, multiple times, as they moved among the lunching ladies. Most of them murmured condolences about Shirley's death, which affirmed what Nancy had said. If these acquaintances knew how much she had cared for her late friend, then perhaps Shirley herself had known it too.

Thirty

THAT evening, John pulled into the garage and entered the house fully prepared to find his wife morose from a day of grieving in solitude. Instead, he found a more upbeat version of his wife than he had seen in weeks. As they settled onto the sofa with their drinks, she described the ten hours since his departure that morning.

"I got a workout, and then my friend Nancy and I took a walk and had lunch. By the time I connected with the pastor this afternoon, she had already spoken with Dick. A memorial service is being planned for Saturday week. The Mayo and Tonto communities are the Harringtons' extended family, and Jean is expecting the church to be full."

Jennifer paused and took a sip of her wine, her expression thoughtful. "She said Dick had suggested I say a few words about Shirley, but I'm not sure. I told her I needed to think about it overnight. I'm honored to be asked, but I've never done anything like that, speaking in front of a crowd, I mean. And I'm afraid of losing my composure."

John murmured to indicate he was listening.

"Oh, and don't think I'm crazy for changing the subject, but I just remembered the funniest thing. It turns out that Nancy is named after Nancy Drew. Her mother was a fan. Apparently, she has her mother's complete set of books." She laughed. "You probably don't even know who that is. Anyway, her husband, Ben, is coming into town this weekend and she wants us all to get together."

"Of course I know who Nancy Drew is. She's right up there with the Hardy Boys and the Bobbsey Twins," John said, laughing too. "What do you know about Ben? If he's a golfer, I'll make a tee time."

"He's an architect. I'm not sure about golf; I know they play pickleball."

John nodded. "We'll figure it out. Did you talk to Dick today? I was thinking maybe we should invite him to join us for dinner, depending on what you have planned, but it's gotten a little late."

"I did that earlier. He asked for a raincheck, said he needed time to be alone. I offered to bring dinner to him, but he said he had things in the fridge. We have leftovers, too, but I'm up for going out if you want a change of scenery."

"Let's have another drink outside and make a plan." John splashed gin and tonic over a fresh ice cube and poured more chardonnay into Jennifer's glass. He led her through the sliding door onto the patio and into the gathering dusk, where they sat quietly, listening to the sounds of the desert.

Thirty-one

TWO nights later Jennifer and John were sitting in the Mesquite Grill with Nancy Scott and Ben Witkowski, having the standard conversation about how each couple had discovered Tonto Verde.

"I never imagined owning a home in Arizona, much less in a gated community," said Ben. "Let's face it, there aren't a lot of Polish Jews here. But then, the more often we came to the desert, the more we liked it, especially in the winter, and, you know, one thing led to another. For now, my presence is required in the office, but it's a puddle-jump from DIA to Phoenix. And Nancy has her writing to keep her busy. I'm sure she doesn't even notice when I'm not here." He laughed as his wife elbowed him in the ribs.

"Those two seem like polar opposites," Jennifer later observed to John, "but somehow a perfect match. I like them both a lot. I haven't had many close friends in my life, you know that. It's like, I don't know, I get to a certain point and then I back away or put up a wall. I feel insecure around other women, like they're somehow better than I am…like, if they really knew me, they wouldn't like me."

She caught her husband's steady, slightly worried gaze, and laughed. "How much do I owe you for this session, Dr. Crouch? Seriously," she continued, "what I'm trying to say is, I want things to be different. If my relationship with Shirley taught me anything, it's that I am worthy of friendship."

She stopped talking and rested her head in the crook of John's arm. He kissed her forehead, and whispered, "I love you, Jeni."

Thirty-two

NANCY Scott arrived at Frank Chavez's office at the appointed time to find him on the phone. He motioned her in and ended his conversation. "Gotta go now. The mystery writer is here to make the rounds with me. She wants to know what a sheriff really does. See you tonight, God willing."

He smiled as he replaced the receiver in its cradle. "My sister," he pointed to one of the pictures behind him. "She's a nurse, works at the Mayo, in Scottsdale. Ready to head out?"

She nodded and followed him from the building, getting into the passenger side of his SUV and fastening her seat belt. "I'm really excited about this," she said. "Thank you, again."

"Glad for the company," he assured her. "Let's stop in at La Casita. It's one of the area's more successful programs for dealing with families in crisis. Eighteen units, two to three bedrooms each, with services on site. It's temporary, with a six-months stay, max. That's not much time to get your life back together when it's fallen apart.

Still, they do a great job. They could help a lot more people if they just had the funding."

"I've heard that Phoenix has one of the largest populations of people experiencing homelessness in the country."

"That's true. It's much worse in the city than here. We do what we can in our little town. Churches pitch in, bring lunches, crafts for the kids. My wife volunteers. She was a social worker before we had our girls."

"I think my friend Jennifer volunteers, too", said Nancy. "Maybe not at the shelter, but I know she makes lunches at her church in Rio Verde, and sometimes delivers them." They pulled into the parking lot of what looked like a normal apartment complex and entered the administration office.

"Good morning, Rosie," Frank said, greeting an attractive dark-haired woman. Nancy wasn't sure whether she was Latina or Native American, or perhaps both. "This is my riding companion, Nancy Scott." The women exchanged smiles and nods. "How's Trevor doing?"

"Back in school, Sheriff," Rosie replied. "So far, so good. Mom got a job at Target. It's a ninety-day trial period, but after that she'll have benefits. She'll need them, to keep him on the meds. We found a volunteer tutor who's good with ADHD kids. He's a retired teacher. He comes four afternoons a week, and he says he sees definite progress. It takes a village…"

"No more bullying?" Frank asked.

"The school resource officer says 'no'. The principal sat down with the offenders and their parents and explained the situation, and it seems that middle school boys can be reasoned with after all. Who would have known? And the two little ones are thriving in full-day kindergarten and pre-school. This family could be one of our poster children, so to speak."

"Great. Keep up the good work, Rosie." Frank tipped his hat and headed toward the door again.

"Hey, thanks for stopping by. It means a lot to us. And nice to meet you, Nancy."

"You, too, Rosie," Nancy said, and followed Frank back out to his truck.

"Wow, that was a surprise!" she exclaimed, after they'd both buckled in. "I had no idea you got involved in situations like this."

"*Involved* is probably too strong a word. But I'd sure rather see our kids get the help they need now than deal with them later in the criminal justice system."

"'Our kids'…you really are a great guy, Frank. Where are you taking me next?" She could tell he was enjoying this almost as much as she was.

"Let's check in with the station and see if we can get someone out of a little trouble," said Frank. He and the dispatcher went back and forth over the intercom until they identified a situation in Rio Verde Foothills that they agreed warranted a visit.

A short time later, Nancy was bouncing around in her seat as they drove down a dirt road. They had entered a sprawling neighborhood of ranch-style houses on half-acre lots, almost every one of them in need of a good handyman and a landscaping service.

Finally, after a few false tries, Frank found the right address. He radioed back to let the dispatcher know he might be going in, then waited with Nancy on the front porch for someone to answer the door.

When no one responded to the bell, or to their knocks, they walked around to the back of the house. All three bays of the triple garage stood open. A rusted-out truck, with its rear license plate hanging by one screw, was parked in the middle. The rest of the space, which didn't appear to have been cleaned in the last decade, was crammed, from floor to ceiling, with tools, old bicycles, lawn maintenance equipment, paint cans, an ancient sewing machine, and stacks of boxes—the type that moving companies use. There was a narrow, dusty path through the garage contents to a back door. Frank took it and rapped loudly. Nancy followed, a few feet behind.

An old man, leaning on a walker, answered the door.

"Good morning, sir. I'm Deputy Chavez, and this is Nancy Scott." He motioned over his shoulder. "Are you Dr. Tucker?"

"Yes. Yes, I am. Is there a problem, Sheriff?"

"Well, we hope not, but your son is worried about you, says he's been calling you for the past two days, and that you haven't answered the phone. If you're safe, I suggest we give him a call right now and let him know."

"My son. Yes, he's over in Chandler, comes to check on me every couple of weeks or so. I didn't know he was calling. I lost my phone, so I got a neighbor to drive me into town to buy a new one, and they convinced me I should also change my service. They couldn't set the new phone up for me, because I didn't have any of my passwords with me. I just found my old phone, but the battery's dead. I don't mind telling you, I'm a little confused."

Frank nodded. "Well, let's call your son first and let him know you're okay, and then I think I can help you get things sorted out. We'll need to plug your old phone in and turn it on. May we please come inside?"

Thirty-three

TWO hours later, Nancy and Frank walked into Phil's Filling Station, which she later described to Ben as "a blast from the past".

"Table or booth?" asked one of waitresses, who was dressed in vintage diner attire. Nancy hesitated, ogling the huge slices of pie displayed in a refrigerated case near the door.

"Lady's choice," Frank said, motioning to Nancy.

"Booth, I think," she decided. She slid into one of the red leatherette seats the waitress led them to.

"Wow, what a menu? What don't they serve here?" she asked.

"And it's all good." Frank beamed at the waitress, whose name, Betty, was embroidered in white on her red polyester shirt. "Better give us a minute." He laughed as Nancy alternated between studying the menu intently, looking out the window at the erupting fountain the town was named for, and scanning the extensive collection of Coca Cola memorabilia on the walls.

"Unbelievable," she said to herself. "Is it too plebeian just to have a hamburger? I mean, I'm overwhelmed."

"The burgers are great," Frank said, motioning that they were ready to order. "But you have to decide which one."

"Oh my gosh! I'll have the mushroom burger, medium, sweet potato fries, diet Coke with lime." Nancy thrust her laminated menu toward the waitress before she had time to change her mind.

"Make it two, Betty. Regular Coke." Frank leaned back in his booth with a broad smile on his face.

"What? What is it, Frank?"

"Nothing, Nancy. Nothing at all. I just can't wait to see the look on your face when you see the size of your meal."

"Uh-oh, what have you gotten me into?" She laughed, then leaned across the table, lowering her voice. "So, seriously Frank, just saying, this little town seems like a pretty darned great place to live. Does violent crime even exist here? I mean, do you ever get to handle a murder investigation?"

"Not if I can help it."

Thirty-four

"TALK about local color, boy did I see it this morning!" Nancy laughed, as she relayed the details of her day to Ben that evening.

"And Frank's a good guy, as good as they say?"

"Better. I can assure you that this part of the county is in great hands. He said the next time I decide to tag along with him, we'll go to the McDowell Yavapai Nation reservation. They do their own policing, but there's a friendly relationship."

"Sounds like you made a pretty good impression on the sheriff."

"He's an easy-going man, but I don't think much gets past him. He has his finger on the pulse of the community, and he seems to truly care about its residents. He's someone you would want to have as a friend, although I suspect he keeps his boundaries. Anyway, super-fun day, and the boost I needed for my book."

"Speaking of, how's it coming?"

"It's coming..." She grinned.

Thirty-five

"**THE** funeral was Saturday, very beautiful. The pastor did a wonderful job of describing Shirley in a way that made me feel sad, but grateful to have known her. I'm happy she's at peace now and reunited with her son. The church was full, and there were so many flowers…"

Jennifer and Nancy were hiking in the park on a day that could only be described as brilliant—the surrounding mountains, jagged and purple in the distance, were juxtaposed against a clear blue sky. The desert was in full bloom and animated with birdsong. A Northern Harrier, a hawk easily identified in flight by its white rump patch, soared overhead. The air was crisp, but that would change, which is why Jennifer had insisted they get an early start.

"Did you speak?" asked Nancy.

Jennifer nodded. "I did, at the graveside service, before the one at the church. It was Dick, John and I, and some other close friends of the Harringtons from Dick's years at the clinic. And the pastor, of course. I just talked about how kind Shirley had been to me when we first moved to Tonto Verde, how close we had become volunteering together and then during her illness, and how, at the end of her life, we were so much more than friends.

"Dick told John that Shirley thought of me like a daughter. Given the relationship, or, I should say, the lack of one, that I had with my mother, it's hard for me to think of Shirley in exactly those terms. I don't know how to explain it, Nancy; I never felt related to my own mother."

"I'm sorry," said Nancy, and Jennifer knew she meant it. Nancy had told her recently that she and her own mother were the best of friends.

"How do you think Dr. Harrington will do without his wife—over time, I mean? Some men just seem lost. Some women do, too, I guess. But we seem to be better at feeding ourselves."

They both laughed.

"I know what you're saying. I don't know. They were married for over fifty years and had been through so much together. Dick was devoted to her care, so there may be a sense of lost purpose. But maybe some relief, too. I'll keep feeding him, if he'll let me. But he'll be lonely, no question."

The path grew steeper, but it was still easy enough to walk and talk at the same time. "By the way, how was your ride with the sheriff?" Jennifer asked.

"It was great; Frank's terrific! A good person for me to model my character after. We visited La Casita. Isn't that where you and the other church ladies volunteer?"

"We make lunches weekly for the residents, yes. And we've collected school supplies, filled backpacks for the kids, that kind of thing. And we plan some special events. There's a "trick or trunk" coming up. Wanna help?"

"Maybe, sounds fun."

After completing the North Trail loop and returning to Tonto Verde through the gate on the eastern border of the park, Jennifer waved goodbye to Nancy and wished her a good day of writing. Then she turned toward home.

John had left for the office, and the house was cool and quiet. The day stretched in front of her like a blank canvas. She wasn't sure exactly what she should do with it. She decided to wait until nine o'clock, and then check in on Dick.

"Good morning," she said, when he picked up at the first ring. "How are you feeling today? The service was beautiful, Dick. I think Shirley would have approved."

"I'm glad to hear you say that, and I agree. How are you and John this morning?"

"I'm fine; I just got back from a hike in the park, and John's at the office. Things have been going well for him, and I know he appreciates the doors you've opened. Will you please join us for dinner tonight? I'm serving my best French cassoulet."

"I may not be the best guest; I'm sure you understand. But I can't resist the thought of that cassoulet. Sounds like it calls for a good Bordeaux, which I can provide. What time would you like me to come?"

"Come around six-thirty. John and I will enjoy your company, regardless of your mood."

Thirty-six

JENNIFER was arranging silverware and wine glasses when John walked through the door. She raised her head for his kiss and smiled brightly—a smile, she thought, he strained to return.

"Everything okay, hon?" she asked, knowing he often needed a little time before he was ready to share.

"It looks like Dick accepted your invitation; that's good," he deflected, gesturing at the three place settings. "Let me freshen up and then we'll talk."

She heard the familiar buzz of his electric shaver, then of his toothbrush, finding both mundane sounds comforting. When he strode back into the kitchen, scented with her favorite aftershave, and headed for the refrigerator, she wondered if her initial reading had been wrong.

John sat on one of the stools at the counter, across from where she was tearing Romaine leaves for a Caesar salad. He took the first sip of his beer and let out a long sigh.

"I got some bad news today," he began, "from the practice manager for those surgeons I've been working with for the last five months."

"Greg?" asked Jennifer. John had indeed been working on this case forever, it seemed, and she knew how badly he wanted to get the business placed.

"Yeah, Greg. He called this afternoon, after we had just put in the order for exams for all the docs. Apparently, one of the newer ones has a brother in the business, and he mentioned he was getting examined for life insurance. The brother doesn't have my experience, not even close, but he's with a reputable company, backed up by some long-term professionals.

"Their products are off-the-shelf, not proprietary like ours, and there's no reason they would choose to go with him instead of me except for the family relationship. The other docs agreed informally to tender another proposal—I mean, it's a lot of money, Jeni—and Greg was in a tough spot. He knows how much time I've put into the design of this program, and he understands the advantage of a firm like McDougal.

"Hopefully it's a temporary setback, but it has me stressed. I've made an amateur's mistake, spending so much of my time on one big case at the expense of pursuing new leads. I know better. God, I hope I don't let you down."

Before Jennifer could reassure him, or ask any questions, the doorbell rang. When she answered it, Dick Harrington stood outside, his arms balancing a stack of clean foil casserole dishes and plastic containers.

Jennifer gave him a teasing look. "I told you these didn't need to be returned," she said.

"I thought you might want to reuse them. I'm not thinking of myself, of course," he smiled, sheepishly.

She relieved him of half the stack and led him inside. "Set those down here and give John your drink order."

"I'll have what you're having, John, and the bottle is fine. Let me run back out to the car and get the wine. I didn't want to take a chance on dropping it."

Dick accepted a beer and sat in the chair Jennifer led him to, sniffing appreciatively. The aroma of pork sausage, poultry, white beans, and herbs filled the small space.

"That smells heavenly," Dick said. "One of the best trips Shirley and I ever took was to the south of France. We were newlyweds. It was between college and med school. The food was amazing, even on our shoestring budget. Especially those rustic country dishes, made with whatever was in season or on hand. We made so many wonderful memories together…"

"She was a gracious and generous woman, Dick, one who touched many lives, if the attendance Saturday is any indication. Jennifer and I loved her too. I know you'll miss her terribly, we all will." John laid his hand briefly on the shoulder of the older man as he stepped across the room to help himself to another beer from the refrigerator.

Jennifer busied herself in the kitchen, enjoying the hum of the men's conversation. It was good for Dick to get out. "Dinner is served," she announced, before too much time had passed, and they all moved to the table.

John had opened the bottle of wine to let it breathe, and now poured it into stemless glasses. "To Shirley", he said, as he sat, and raised his glass. "We were blessed to know her."

"To Shirley," they said in unison.

The poignant moment ended with the clash of glass on china.

Dick stared down at his upended wine glass, which rested in the middle of his dinner plate. "Wait a minute, what just happened? I'm so sorry, Jennifer, it just slipped out of my hand." He dabbed at the wine that had splattered onto his place mat with his napkin, which just happened to be red.

"No worries, Dick. No one's hurt and nothing's broken." Jennifer removed the mess. "I'll get you a fresh plate, and John will get you another glass," she said.

She was back in a minute, with a new plate of cassoulet and a reassuring smile for Dick. The meal continued without further mishap, and Jennifer was warmed by the compliments both men paid to her cooking. As they ate, Jennifer asked Dick if he had any plans. "Travel, I mean, or anything work related. I know they still rely on your expertise at the clinic."

Dick waved off her words. "Not really, they just try to make me feel important. To answer your question, the only thing on my calendar, other than the standing Thursday tee time I've missed too often of late, is a visit to my primary care physician. I was due for a physical when Shirley got sick, and I postponed it. Not a good idea at my age.

"I have some old friends—all widowers—who are taking a riverboat cruise down the Mississippi next spring. They've invited me to join them. For some reason it doesn't appeal. But I may decide to tag along…" He shrugged his shoulders.

"A bunch of guys on a riverboat sounds like fun to me," said John. "Ask if there's room for one more. Just kidding. I need to work, and when I *am* able to get away, Jennifer is long overdue a vacation. Aren't you, Jeni?" He smiled at her.

She returned his smile and rose to remove the dinner plates. "Who would like some warm peach cobbler with vanilla ice cream?" she asked rhetorically.

Thirty minutes later, Dick kissed Jennifer lightly on the cheek and thanked her profusely for the meal and the hospitality. He patted John on the back. "See you the day after tomorrow, my friend, ten before eight. It'll be good to get back on the course."

Thirty-seven

TWO evenings later, Jennifer and John drove toward Nancy and Ben's for cocktails, after which the four of them planned to drive into town for sushi.

"How was golf?" Jennifer asked.

"I shot an eighty-five," John responded, "not bad for a guy who's past his prime. Our friend Dick seemed to be struggling. Of course, he's missed a lot of rounds lately, but he's still a good golfer. There were a couple of times today when he dropped the club he was holding. It seemed to slip right out of his grasp. And it looked like he was having trouble placing his ball, you know, on the tee, and on the green. Probably just nerves, he's been through a lot. His score wasn't that bad, and he is eighty-three, after all."

"He's such a sweetheart," Jennifer said, as John pulled up in front of their friends' home. "We just need to keep including him, make sure he isn't over there alone in that big house too much of the time."

"Yeah, I think he was having dinner at the clubhouse with the Yarboroughs tonight. Dick's one of those guys everybody enjoys having around."

Nancy flung open the door before they could even ring the bell. "You're here, come in! Ben's still in the shower, but he'll be right out. He took a long ride through the park today, dusty, sweaty mess of a man, I almost had to hose him off outside on the patio before letting him inside, do either of you bike?" she paused for breath.

Jennifer laughed at Nancy's usual ebullient chatter. "We own bikes, but they're old ones, not fit for the desert. You might see us pedaling around the neighborhood on occasion. I'll be the one trying to keep up."

Nancy pointed to a bucket of ice with several Japanese beers, and a bottle of sauvignon blanc, sitting on the counter between the kitchen and the dining room. A bowl of wasabi snack mix and some cocktail napkins were nearby. "Keeping with the theme for the evening," she said, "but we have whatever you'd like. Please help yourself." She raised her own, half-filled wine glass.

Jennifer accepted the glass of wine John poured for her. He opened a bottle of beer for himself. Ben entered the room wearing pressed chinos and a Hawaiian print shirt. He shook hands with John and gave Jennifer a peck on the cheek. "I see you've found the bar."

John raised his bottle in assent. "Great place you have here. Looks like an architect's house."

"Want a tour?"

"Sure!" they said in unison. Jennifer loved seeing other people's homes.

"Your instinct is good—this house was built by an architect. To be honest with you, I didn't have to do that much, just a coat of paint and new window coverings. I'm not much into remodeling, too hard on a marriage," he said, with a chuckle. "This won't take long. You're looking at the kitchen and the common space. All that's left are the bedrooms."

Ben led them down a short hallway that branched into matching bedroom suites, each featuring a king bed with matching side tables, and a chair and ottoman. The beds were dressed in various layers and textures in shades of taupe and beige. The lighting was built in, and the floors featured tribal-patterned rugs in muted colors. The bathrooms had skylights and earth-toned countertops, and the showers were walk-ins. The towels were plush, and snowy white. It all looked like a spread out of *Architectural Digest*. The only hint as to which room was slept in regularly was a terrycloth robe lying across one of the beds.

Such a neutral palette for a fireball like Nancy. Who knows how excitable she might be in a home full of primary colors?

"It's beautiful", Jennifer said, "very soothing."

"Thanks", said Ben. "We like it. It's a relaxing space for Nancy to write, and for me to commute to, and we have the spare bedroom for visiting snowbirds. Our laptops are our office."

"Hey, guys, I'm getting hungry! And it would be nice to get to Oka in time to see the fountain erupt," said Nancy.

They drained their glasses and headed to the car, the men opening doors for the women to climb into the back seat. "I feel like we've known each other all our lives," observed Jennifer, as John pulled away from the driveway and drove toward the turn onto Forest Road.

Thirty-eight

"HOW'S the insurance business treating you these days?" Ben asked. "That *is* your business, right? All I know about insurance is that you've gotta have it."

"Insurance and investments," John responded. "And you have the important part down. As to my business, it's fine. There's a case I've been working on for months that's giving me heartburn, but that's the way it goes. The deals aren't done until they're done, you know? So, it's stressful at times. But things have always turned out for us, right Jeni?" He met her eyes in the rearview mirror for a split second, then looked back toward the road. "Or, almost always. So, I try not to let it get to me, take it one day at a time. How about you, what are you working on?"

"We typically have a custom home or two in the office—right now we have one, but it's a big project. I'm personally working on a small medical office building. Doctors, yikes. It's tough getting them to sit down with you."

"I feel your pain," said John.

"And, we have ongoing tenant finish work for a regular client," Ben continued. "It's an insurance company by the way—Secure Alliance. Ever heard of 'em?"

"You bet, good company. Very active in the physicians' market," John said, thinking of the beneficiary change his back office had made for the Harringtons. "Excellent client service…"

"They're good people," Ben agreed.

John turned left onto Palisades Boulevard, and left again onto Avenue of the Fountains, pulling into a parking place right in front of the restaurant. As the hostess seated them and handed them Oka Sushi's list of the chef's daily specialty rolls, the fountain shot three hundred feet into the air, on the hour, as always.

Thirty-nine

"Dick, it's me," Jennifer said into her phone several weeks later, after getting Dick Harrington's recorded message. "I'm making a yummy dish called 'Chicken with Green Chilies and Hominy' for dinner tonight, and I want to bring some over to you. I'd suggest you come here and eat with us, but I'm not sure when John will be home. He has a late afternoon meeting. I'll bring it around four-thirty. If you aren't there, I'll let myself in and leave it in the fridge, okay? You can just heat a serving of it in the microwave. I hope you're out on the golf course having fun. See you later."

Jennifer busied herself around the condo while the chicken for the casserole cooked. She made the bed and threw a load of towels into the machine. Then, she hurried to brush her teeth and apply sunscreen to her arms and face. Nancy would be here any minute for a walk.

"Hey, girl." She heard the now familiar greeting. "You ready to burn some calories?" Nancy poked her head around the front door, which Jennifer had left open for her.

"Coming." Jennifer grabbed her key, and they headed out. "What's on your calendar today?"

"Same old, same old. Putting words on paper. That book's not going to write itself, as they say. You?"

"I'm making one of my favorite southwestern dishes, and taking a few servings to our good friend, Dick."

"How's he doing? And how are *you* doing?"

"Dick's doing as well as can be expected. We all miss Shirley terribly. Toward the end of her life, before she went back to the hospital, I was with her almost every day. She told me a lot about herself, perhaps some things she hadn't told anyone else. I'm a different person for having known her."

"How so?"

"Well, for starters, I can't believe I'm sharing this with you. That's part of what Shirley did for me, let me know it's okay to be who I really am and not who I think people want me to be. She didn't say that in so many words, but she always reassured me it was okay when I thought I had told her too much about my personal life. Pretty basic stuff, huh? I'm mean, you seem to be perfectly comfortable in your own skin."

Nancy was silent for a beat, then nodded. "Yeah, I think I am. My mom was into all that 'free to be you and me' stuff, always encouraging me to be my authentic self. Anyway, I sure like who you really are—no telling who I'd be hanging out with if we hadn't met each other that day at Lady Putters. And Ben and I both like John. The four of us are going to have lots of fun here in the desert, I just know it!"

They walked for a while in silence, unusual for Nancy. Maybe she was plotting a scene in her book. A roadrunner crossed their path ahead, and a covey of quails dispersed into the brush.

It's beautiful here. A sense of contentment filled Jennifer's soul. She welcomed the feeling; it was one that had too often eluded her.

Forty

JENNIFER came into the living room and found John slumped in his favorite chair, staring blankly out the window.

"You're home early," she said, "your meeting…"

"Cancelled," he said, turning to her with a look of despair. "At the last minute. I was supposed to meet with the docs. I planned to review my current proposal with them and compare it to the other guy's, and they were going to make a decision. I mean, every day they don't do anything is another day they're exposed; I've tried to impress that urgency on Greg.

"He called after lunch with a lame excuse about one of the docs needing to pick up his kids at school because his wife got sick. I mean, seriously, don't these guys have nannies? They're surgeons, for God's sake. He didn't even have the decency to tell me directly. He left the message with the front desk. When I called him back, the receptionist said he was in a meeting and put me through to his voice mail. I left a message asking to reschedule with them, but I never heard back. I couldn't hang around the office, didn't trust my emotions. James McDougal knew I was meeting with them—knew we were close…" He covered his face with his hands. "Oh, Jeni, I'm afraid this is slipping away from us, and I don't have much else in the pipeline."

Jennifer hadn't seen her husband this negative since their financial debacle almost fourteen years earlier. It was unsettling. Still, even caught in the grip of all that loss, and as despondent as he had been, he had assured her that he would make it back, that he would do whatever was required to take care of her, and she had believed him. She still believed him. Somehow, he would make it happen. That was the kind of man John was.

The two sat in silence, until the oven timer went off. Jennifer got up to turn it off, and stayed in the kitchen, where she constructed an entree for her and John, and one for Dick. She also made two salads, one in a wooden bowl and one in a plastic container. Next, she cut a long loaf of French bread in half, sliced each of the halves, and spread the slices with butter. She sprinkled on some garlic salt and sealed the pieces in foil.

Should she invite Dick to dinner, since John had come home after all? The two men enjoyed each other's company, and she often thought Dick had a mellowing effect on John. Suddenly she had an even better idea.

"Honey, I've made our dinner, and enough for Dick, too. He's expecting me to bring it to him about now, but I need to make a phone call to La Casita about our food delivery tomorrow. Could I get you to run it over there?"

Maybe he'll invite you in for a beer and maybe talking to an older man who has been through a lot will help put this setback in perspective.

"Sure, babe, I can do that," John answered without enthusiasm, "just give me a few minutes." He dragged himself out of his chair and disappeared into the bathroom, where Jennifer heard the water running and the hum of the electric toothbrush.

When he came back into the living room, he was wearing a golf shirt and shorts, and the change seemed to Jennifer to have carried over to his outlook. She went to him and put her arms around him. He held her close and nuzzled her neck before kissing her deeply.

"Things will be okay," she said, gently pulling away. "You've always taken good care of me, no matter what. Remind Dick, a three-fifty oven for about fifteen minutes, or a zap of the microwave, is all this should need. Feel free to stay if he asks you to visit. There's no rush."

John set the items on the floor of the golf cart and waved goodbye as he backed out of the garage. As he passed, Jennifer thought she detected the hint of a smile.

Forty-one

THE next morning Jennifer arrived early at Christ Church in the Desert. She had volunteered to transport the lunches they made weekly into Fountain Hills and wanted to ask a couple of the women if they had any interest in going with her and having lunch afterward. She had become fond of this group of volunteers Shirley had introduced her to. Several of them were, if not friends, close acquaintances on the way to becoming friends. In the weeks that followed Shirley's death, they had been a source of support, and sharing her grief with them had made it more bearable.

The pastor was also a comfort, and these days she and John often made their way to church—which started at nine— before heading off to other Sunday activities. This was new for them both. Neither had grown up in any faith tradition, though they both claimed to believe in a higher power. They had nothing to compare this experience to, didn't even know the right questions to ask. But since Shirley's death, the idea of her being reunited with the son she had lost, and the concept of an afterlife, had become compelling for Jennifer.

As people arrived, they expressed surprise at seeing her there. "Have I missed something?" she asked.

"You haven't heard," said a man named Ed. It was a statement, rather than a question.

"Heard what?"

"Dick Harrington. When the cleaning lady arrived this morning, she found him dead."

Jennifer grabbed the back of a chair as her legs threatened to fold. "Rosario? Found Dick dead?" She shook her head. "But we just took supper to him last night. I mean, John took it. Dick was fine. I mean, he wasn't there, so John thought he must have gone over to the clubhouse for a beer with one of the fellows. John left the food in the refrigerator. We have the garage code. The car was there. I don't know about the golf cart…" Jennifer felt herself becoming a little hysterical.

"Excuse me," she murmured, and plunged through the double doors to the breezeway. She hit the number for John she had programmed into her phone. He answered immediately.

"John!" She burst into tears.

"I know, Jeni. I've been trying to call you—you must have forgotten to take your phone out of silent mode this morning. Gary sent a group text to our regular foursome. I read it when I got to the parking lot, and I called him. He was—probably still is—at the Harringtons."

"But what happened? Dick was fine when you went over yesterday, right?"

"I don't actually know that, Jeni. I let myself in, remember? I assumed he was over at the clubhouse, or maybe on the putting green. Apparently the cleaning lady, Rosie…"

"Rosario," Jennifer corrected.

"She arrived this morning at eight and saw Dick sitting in the hot tub. She figured he was just taking an early morning soak, something he often did. But she went outside to ask him about something, and he was unconscious. She called nine-one-one, and then she called the Yarboroughs—she works for them, too. By the time Gretchen and Gary got there, the fire department had already arrived. The paramedic declared Dick dead at the scene. It's presumed to be a heart attack."

"Where did they take him?"

"I don't know. I assume he's still at his house, or maybe at the funeral home? Look, Jeni, I'm just walking into a meeting. I'll come home as soon as it's over. I'm sorry, honey. This is a lot to handle, but I don't really think there's anything you or I can do at the moment."

They hung up and Jennifer returned to the church fellowship hall, where the assembly line was now set up for the usual routine. Everyone was talking about the Harringtons, but no one had much information—only what Ed had already said. She decided to keep what little she knew to herself. She would take the lunches into Fountain Hills, turn around, and come home. Hopefully, by then, John would be there.

Forty-two

AFTER dropping off one hundred neatly organized lunch sacks at La Casita, Jennifer headed back through Fountain Hills toward McDowell Mountain Road. While she was stopped briefly at the light at Palisades and Fountain Hills Boulevard, she scrolled down the display screen in her car and touched Nancy's number. Immediately she received the formatted text reply "I'll call you back". A few minutes later her phone rang.

"Jennifer? You've heard the news about Dr. Harrington, I'm sure. I'm so sorry. I know what good friends you are—were, I mean."

"I just can't believe it…"

"It seems to have caught everyone by surprise, although he is, I mean he was, eighty-three years old. Listen, I'm actually here now."

"Where?"

"At the Harringtons. I was supposed to spend the morning with Frank Chavez, to meet him in town and make his rounds with him again. But the district called to say he was driving out to Tonto, and I could meet him here if I wanted to. I had no idea…"

"Is he still there? Dick, I mean?"

"Yes, but I don't think for too much longer. Obviously, I've stayed outside. The funeral home people are here. You'll have a chance to say goodbye when they get him, you know, ready. At least, I assume there will be a viewing, you know, before his funeral? I guess that may all be up to his attorney. He's here, too.

"I guess there's no family, is that right? Listen, I feel very sorry for your loss. Can you and John come over later? I'll make something easy for dinner. We can sit out on the patio when it cools off. Ben is in Denver, so it will just be the three of us."

"That would be nice…" Jennifer managed to get out, before she lost her connection in the desert.

Forty-three

"THANK God, you're home," Jennifer said, launching herself at John when he walked through the garage door at two o'clock. "I've been pacing the floor. I feel like I should be doing something, but I don't know what to do. I haven't had lunch, but I'm not even hungry. I called Pastor Jean and got her voice mail. She called me back and said she'd had a call from the funeral home." She slipped out of his arms and began to pace.

"Of course, she had already heard the news this morning, at the church. She invited me to come to her office tomorrow morning, for a cup of coffee. She said there would be a service, but she wasn't sure when. I guess she's waiting to hear from someone named 'Al,' who's representing Dick."

"Al Farnsworth, Dick's attorney. I met him when I took the beneficiary change form over for Dick and Shirley to sign." John raised his hand to his forehead. "Oh my God, Jeni, the life insurance. The policy pays off at the second death, Dick's death. One million dollars. To you. Jesus Christ."

Forty-four

"GIRLS, how's the homework coming?" Margaret Chavez stepped around the corner from the kitchen to check on Scottie and Ginny, who were sprawled out on the living room floor in front of their laptops. The television streamed Olivia Rodrigo at a moderate volume in the background. "Aunt Maria is coming for dinner tonight. You can set the table when you're finished."

"Aunt Maria? Awesome!" The twins high-fived each other. "I'm almost done," added Ginny.

"Me too," Scottie said.

"Great. She gets off work at five. With traffic she should be here by five-thirty. Your dad should be home about the same time. Dinner plates, water glasses, knives and forks, napkins…"

Margaret glanced over at her mother-in-law. Aurelia sat in her reading chair, alternating between turning the pages of an old issue of *Latina* magazine and dozing. The deep creases in her coffee-colored skin belied her relative youth. She was only fifty-five years old, but the first forty had been difficult.

An hour later Frank entered the kitchen from the back door, hanging his hat on a peg Margaret had put there for that purpose. He walked over to her and put his hands on her shoulders as she stood stirring something in a saucepan, turning her around gently and lifting her chin. "That smells divine," he said, after their lips parted company. "What is it?"

"Mushroom gravy, for a meatloaf. Roasted potatoes and salad on the side. And, drumroll please, a homemade cherry pie." She smiled modestly.

"Wow, I know my sister's coming. Is she bringing Princess Kate?"

"As though I don't cook great meals for you every night! Actually, I invited her to bring June, but she had a date, I think. Would you go see if the girls have started setting the table, please?"

"What have you two juvenile delinquents been up to today?" Frank teased, as his daughters ran to hug his waist. He put an arm around each of them and pulled them close, then released them and walked toward his mother, whose eyelids were now closed.

"Mamá, como estas? Te quiero." Frank spoke softly, and kissed the top of his mother's head.

"Cómo estuvo tu día?" she asked, opening her eyes and looking up at her son.

"Bien, bien," he responded to her inquiry about his day. "They haven't fired me yet," he added, with a wink.

From the kitchen he heard laughter, and the sound of the ice machine as it dropped cubes into glasses the girls pushed against the refrigerator door. Occasionally, they failed to release the pressure fast enough, and he could hear the ice spilling onto the floor, eliciting more laughter. He smiled as he headed down the hall to change out of his uniform and into his jeans. He sidetracked into the bathroom and splashed cold water onto his face. "You are one lucky man," he reminded his reflection.

Frank returned to the living room as his sister came through the front door.

"Hola, Hermano!" she said, as she made a beeline for their mother and planted a kiss on her cheek.

She gave Frank a hug and headed toward the kitchen with the bottle of wine she had brought. Frank followed her in. As soon as she set the bottle down, she was embraced by the twins and surrounded by a cascade of giggles.

"You two get prettier every time I see you—and smarter too, I assume. You are going to take the world by storm."

"Let's have a glass of this right now, shall we?" Margaret said, nodding toward the bottle of wine. "Or would you rather have a cocktail?"

"Wine's good," Maria said. "I can sure use it tonight."

Frank removed the cork and poured three inches of wine into each of two glasses. He handed a glass to his wife and one to his sister. "What made your day so tough?"

"It was more sad than tough," said Maria. "Our dear Dr. Harrington died last night. Or maybe this morning, I'm not sure. Anyway, he was like a patron saint at the clinic, and we'll miss him terribly. Did you hear about it?"

Frank grabbed a beer out of the refrigerator. "I did," he said, as he twisted off the bottle cap. "In fact, I took the call and went out to Tonto Verde this morning. The EMTs alerted us a little after eight. The housekeeper found him, in the hot tub. Heart attack, apparently. I guess he lost his wife recently. Sounds like they were pillars of the community."

"Was he old?" Ginny asked.

"What kind of doctor was he?" Her sister chimed in.

"He was a cardiologist—that's a heart doctor," answered their aunt. "He was in his eighties and had been with the Mayo since he was a young surgeon. Everyone loved him. He took an interest in getting to know even the lowest level employee. He was so kind; sometimes he would sit down next to someone waiting in the reception area just to say a few comforting words. His death was unexpected. Although, we shouldn't be shocked. No one lives forever. Now, tell your Tia Maria what's new at school and on the soccer field."

The girls began talking at once to their aunt, as Margaret carried platters of food to the dining room. Frank gently roused his mother, who had again nodded off, and led her to her place at the table.

After holding Margaret's chair, Frank seated himself next to her at the head of the table and bowed his head. "Señor Dios, Padre celestial: Bendícenos y bendice estos tus dones, que de tu gran bondad recibimos. Por Jesucristo, nuestro Señor."

"Amen," his family said in unison.

Forty-five

"**Come** in, you two," Nancy exclaimed as she hugged Jennifer, then John. He handed her a bottle of cold chardonnay.

"Thank you, let's open that right now. There's beer in the fridge for you. Or would you prefer something stronger? I'm so sorry about your friend. What a tough time you two have had. First Mrs. Harrington, and now her husband. Ben sends his love. He wishes he were here."

"Would you please tell me everything that happened this morning?" Jennifer asked, accepting a glass of wine.

"Of course, sit down. I'll tell you everything I know. As I said, I was supposed to go into Fountain Hills this morning to the sheriff's office. But the receptionist, who I met when I went in before, called me about eight-thirty and said not to come, that Frank wouldn't be there. She said he was on his way to Tonto Verde and had left word that I could meet him out here if I liked. She gave me an address and told me to wait outside when I got there. When I put it into my app, it was so close I decided to walk. There was a firetruck in front of the house, and an ambulance, and Frank's SUV and another car. While I waited, a woman came outside. She seemed very upset."

"Rosario?"

"Yes, that was her name. I guess she had come to clean the house for Dr. Harrington—I soon learned whose home it was—and saw him sitting in the hot tub. She went out to talk to him and saw that he was unconscious. She didn't know he was dead. She called nine-one-one, and then she called some friends of the Harringtons whom she also cleans for."

"Gretchen and Gary Yarborough," said John.

"Yes," said Nancy. "The fire department down on Forest Road responded first, even before the Yarboroughs. But Dr. Harrington was already dead. The firemen called Frank, and he called the medical examiner in Scottsdale to meet him there. I guess it takes a doctor to certify a death in Arizona. The Yarboroughs called the funeral home, and the funeral home called Dr. Harrington's attorney."

"Al Farnsworth," volunteered John.

"Exactly. And soon, he showed up. So, at that point, it was a cast of thousands. But everything happened in an orderly fashion, which—please don't take this the wrong way—is very helpful information for my book. The sheriff invited me in at this point. We examined the scene, looked all around the house, inside and out, and he officially determined there was no reason to suspect anything other than natural causes, which is what the medical examiner put on his report.

"The funeral home took Dr. Harrington's body, and Mr. Farnsworth told Rosario he would like her to start packing up the Harringtons' personal belongings as soon as she felt up to it, so that he could list the house for sale. They have some beautiful things, as you know. I don't know how it works when there's no family. I guess maybe he'll call in an appraiser and sell them on consignment, or maybe send them to an auction house? I don't think they do garage sales here in Tonto. It's strange to think of someone not having anyone…"

Jennifer sat quietly on the sofa, wiping away tears. John sat beside her, squeezing her free hand.

"When I said I would make you a simple supper, I wasn't kidding. I'm putting a couple of frozen pizzas into the oven and opening a bag of salad. And we have plenty of wine," Nancy said, as she moved toward the kitchen.

Forty-six

"**I'M** working from home today," John announced the following morning, as he placed a cup of coffee and a shortbread cookie on Jennifer's bedside table.

"Are you sure?" she asked drowsily, arranging her pillows against the headboard, and reaching for the steaming mug. "I'm okay, really, I am. But I'm glad you'll be here, and I promise not to disturb you. I can't bring myself to putt this morning, and I couldn't anyway. I'm meeting Jean.

"All the ladies will be talking about Dick, and they'd want to know how much I know about his death, which is more than any of them most likely, except perhaps Gretchen. I still can't believe it, John. I barely slept last night, and when I did, I had the weirdest dreams. The thing I'm struggling with is that no one survives them. There isn't anyone to express our condolences to. It feels like a huge void—a big, black hole."

"It isn't the natural order of things," said John, "to have your children die before you do."

They fell into silence then, sipping their coffee. *This is the way it will be when we die.* John didn't dare voice this prediction out loud, not at a time like this.

"Jeez, who's calling me this early?" His phone vibrated against his bedside table.

"John Crouch?"

"Yes." He walked into the living room with the phone to his ear.

"Sorry to call so early. Al Farnsworth here. So sorry for your loss. For our loss, I should say. Dick Harrington was a longtime friend, and a prince of a man. It was a privilege to know him, and it's a privilege to be tasked with tying up his affairs."

"'A prince of a man.' No truer words were ever spoken," John said. "My wife and I had only known him a little over a year, but we will miss him greatly. She's feeling especially bereft. Is there something I can help with, Al?"

"Your wife was very close to Shirley. Their housekeeper is going to begin packing things up soon—Goodwill, consignment and so on, depending on the value. If there's anything Jennifer—did I get that right?"

"Yes, Jennifer is my wife."

"Well, if there's anything Jennifer would like to have, according to a personal memorandum they left with their copy of the wills, she's free to claim it, now that Dick's gone. Any of Shirley's personal effects, household furnishings, jewelry—that kind of thing. I'll be sending someone out to do an inventory, but Jennifer may go on over and select anything she would like to keep. You can let me know what she chooses."

Once again, John was blown away by the Harringtons' generosity. "Okay. Thanks, Al."

"Sure. Anything with a title is owned in a trust. To be honest, in all my years of estate work, I've never had clients who left no heirs, no family members, I mean. Settling disputes—that I'm used to. And it's the damnedest things kids fight over. I could tell you some stories. Anyway, I just wanted to give you the heads up."

"I'll tell Jeni. I'm sure that having something to remember Shirley by will be very meaningful for her. And," John cleared his throat, "at the risk of sounding callous, what about the life insurance claim?"

"Yeah, we'll get to that as soon as we have the death certificate. My paralegal handles those. She'll be in touch. We submit the claim, they process it within a few weeks, sometimes less, sometimes more, depending. These days, the insurance companies don't send a check, they send a checkbook. They try to keep the funds on deposit as long as they can. You know how it works. They pay interest on them, try to sell the beneficiary an annuity or some other investment, anything to keep the money in the family, so to speak.

"Yes. Well, please let me know if there's anything I can do to help."

"Will do, John. Sorry again for calling so early. Bye now."

John walked back into the bedroom and sat down next to Jennifer.

"What was that all about?" she asked.

He relayed the details of the conversation.

"How kind of them," she said. She pushed the covers back and got out of the bed. "I'd better get ready for my meeting with Jean." She disappeared into the bathroom and closed the door.

John sat with his coffee and tried to organize his thoughts. On the one hand, he had the business deal he was still hoping to save, one that would earn him a big production bonus. On the other hand, his wife was going to be receiving a checkbook with a million plus dollars in it. Either one of these financial events, and certainly a combination of the two, would go a long way toward restoring their losses—his losses, if he was to be totally honest—of fourteen years ago.

Jennifer emerged, and he rose to take her in his arms. "God, I love you, Jeni. How did I get so lucky? And you smell so good…" He nuzzled her neck, stirring with a sudden and strong desire for her.

"Hmmm," she pulled away slightly, and took his face in her hands, rough with its twenty-four-hour stubble. "You're working from home today, are you? Well, why don't you shave, and then try to be productive while I go meet with the pastor, and then maybe I'll come into your office and seduce you. How does that sound?"

It sounded like an offer he wouldn't refuse.

Forty-seven

WHEN Jennifer arrived at Christ Church in the Desert at nine o'clock, there was already a buzz of activity. A men's Bible study group, a women's sewing circle making layettes for babies born to incarcerated mothers, and a small group of volunteers stuffing flyers into the coming Sunday's bulletins, were just a few of the events taking place throughout the building. The church membership was mostly composed of retired folks, people who had led impressive and fruitful lives and still had talent and energy to spare.

Jennifer greeted the church administrator, whom she knew from her volunteer work on Tuesdays, and told her she was there to meet Pastor Jean. She accepted the cup of coffee she was offered and waited until the pastor emerged from her office. Jean hugged Jennifer, and invited her in.

"How are you today?" Jean asked.

Jennifer wasn't sure if she could put how she felt into words. "I'm okay, I guess. I didn't sleep well last night. It's all just so sudden. I mean, we—John and I—just saw Dick recently, and he seemed fine." A sudden image from their last evening together bubbled up. "Well, except for…" She shook her head. "Nothing really, he did seem fine. He was his same wonderful, kind self, even though I know he was missing Shirley terribly. I keep thinking that maybe he died of a broken heart." She shook her head sadly.

"You were very close to her, I know."

"Yes, very close. She was like a best friend, or a big sister. I never had either of those."

The pastor nodded her head.

"I was an only child, and we moved around a lot when I was growing up. I didn't have the chance, or rather, I never took advantage of the opportunity, to become close to any of the girls at school. I felt embarrassed about my home life, and it was easier being on the outside of things when I made it my choice. I'm only now realizing how much I missed out on."

"That must have been lonely," Jean said.

"It was. But after high school, I met John, and we became a twosome. John is my rock. I don't know what I would do without him. But I know women friends are important too, and when I met Shirley, and she invited me into her world, I had this sense of belonging that I hadn't ever felt before. I really did love her, and Dick, too. They were wonderful to me, and I wish I had told them just how much they meant to me."

"Don't you imagine they knew that? When we care deeply for people, they can usually tell."

"I hope so. I felt so sorry for them, having lost their only son. Richie was just a little younger than I am. I wish there was something I could do to honor their memories—all three of them, including Richie, who of course I never knew."

"I understand, and I'm betting an idea comes to you. Use me as a sounding board if you like. In the short term, there's going to be a service here for Dick a week from Saturday. It would be nice to have some family photos, and maybe some memorabilia. Do you have access to these things, and if so, would you be willing to put a small display together?

"One of the Mayo doctors, who worked with Dick for years and who worships here, is going to write a few paragraphs for the bulletin, and speak about him at the service. He's provided a professional portrait. Dick never boasted, but as I'm sure you know, he was renowned in his field, and beloved in the Verde and Mayo communities."

"And he was a great golfer, according to John."

"Yes, that too."

"I'll be glad to do what I can," said Jennifer. "Thank you for asking me. It feels good to be able to contribute."

PART THREE

Forty-eight

"HEY, Jack, how's it going?" Nancy Scott plopped onto a bar stool at the Mesquite Grill and opened her laptop, planning to work on revisions to her novel.

"Living the dream, Nancy. What'll it be? The usual?"

"Please," she responded, as the bartender reached for the Grey Goose and poured a jigger of the syrupy vodka into a cocktail shaker. She smiled, imperceptibly licking her lips, as he added cranberry juice, simple syrup, and ice, then shook the ingredients vigorously for fifteen seconds. She admired the perfect Cosmopolitan placed before her, a thin slice of lime garnishing the rim of the stemmed glass, then raised it in a toast to its creator.

"Cheers," she said.

"Cheers back at you. How's the book coming? Ready to tell me the name yet?"

"As a matter of fact, I am. The working title is *A Murder at Rancho Manana*, and I think I'm sticking with that."

"Rancho Manana, eh? I tended bar there one season. Filled in when they lost their main guy, not to murder, of course." He laughed. "Nice place. More than a few crazies in Cave Creek, though. Lots of motorcycle gangs, *clubs*, I should say, right? So, who gets killed?"

"You'll have to read the book, Jack." She gave him a wink. "Don't worry, I'll bring you a copy."

"I don't read a lot of books, but I'll read yours. Especially if you sign it."

"You got it!" Nancy stumbled into this sort of conversation every now and again, and it always gave her a sense of satisfaction. She sipped her drink and smiled at the only other person in the bar, a man drinking a Stella from the bottle a few stools down.

The man smiled back. "You're a mystery writer, is that correct? I'm sorry for eavesdropping."

"I am."

"Mind if I join you? I'm working on a little mystery myself."

"Not at all. I'm Nancy Scott." She thrust out her hand.

"Ken Carlisle. Do you live here in Tonto Verde?"

"For the past six months. My husband commutes between here and Denver. We have a home there, too." Better get that fact on the table, she thought, as she realized she had removed her wedding ring earlier for a quick manicure and forgotten to put it back on.

"Ever meet a doctor by the name of Richard Harrington?"

"Not exactly…" Nancy's naturally suspicious, fiction-writing mind kicked into high gear. Who was this guy? "I know who he was. I think everyone in this community does."

"What do they say he died of?"

She did a double take. "Natural causes. He was in his eighties." She took a sip of her icy Cosmo and decided to cut to the chase. "Does Dr. Harrington's death have something to do with the mystery you're working on?"

"It does. I investigate insurance claims. This one is for a Denver-based company, Secure Alliance."

Nancy nodded. "My husband has done some work for them. He's an architect. But why are you investigating Dr Harrington's death?"

"There was a beneficiary change made to his life insurance policy just months before his death. A person he couldn't have known for very long is due to receive a lot of money. It's a bit unusual, so the company asked me to look into it."

"Who is this person…the one receiving the money, I mean?"

He shook his head. "I've said too much already. Just wondered if you knew the good doctor."

"No, but I wish I had. I've heard he was very generous. Maybe he just really liked this person…" An uncomfortable thought had intruded. *It couldn't be, could it?* "Oh my gosh, I just remembered I have a delivery to sign for—don't want to miss it. Better go, nice meeting you."

She slammed her laptop closed and hurried out of the bar, leaving her half-filled glass for the bartender to clear away.

Forty-nine

"**I'M** coming, I'm coming." Jennifer hurried to answer the front door, wiping her hands on her apron as she went. When she opened it, a breathless Nancy fell in. "What…?"

"Jennifer, what do you know about Dr. Harrington and a big life insurance policy?"

Jennifer stepped behind her and shut the door. "Come sit down in the living room. Can I pour you a glass of wine?" She pulled an open bottle from the refrigerator and filled two glasses without waiting for an answer. "What brought this up?"

Nancy sat down on the couch and set her untouched wine on the coffee table. "Please, just tell me everything—it's important."

Confused, Jennifer sat down next to her friend. Nancy always had a lot of energy, but this was over the top, even for her. "It's simple really, though I admit, kind of shocking. Dick showed up at John's office one day and told him that he and Shirley had a policy that would pay after they both died. He said they wanted to change it so that I would receive half the money. Shirley was sick then, but Dick was fine, and, as I said, it didn't pay until they both passed, so we thought, ten, fifteen, maybe twenty years from now. Then Shirley died, and now Dick has died. I should be receiving the money any day, according to their attorney. I didn't mean to keep this from you, but it sounded like bragging to tell you. And John said we should be discreet about how we got the money. How *did* you hear, anyway?"

"You're not going to like this, but there's a private investigator here in TV, asking questions. I just happened to run into him at the bar, and he asked if I knew Dr. Harrington, and what I thought about how he died. He's looking into things for the insurance company that wrote the policy, specifically about the beneficiary change. Normally, I don't think an investigator would disclose this much." Nancy raised a finger to her chin. "Now that I think about it, I wonder if he knows you and I are friends. Maybe he wants me to tell you, in the hopes you'll misstep."

Jennifer shook her head. "Misstep how? I haven't done any-thing wrong."

Nancy patted her knee. "I know you haven't. I'm just warning you. I don't know, girl; this guy made my antennae go up, for sure."

"But what should I do?"

"I don't know there's anything you can do, just be aware. I don't know how much money we're talking about, but whether it's fifty cents or five hundred million, I'm in your corner. And by the way, my big news? There's an agent who's interested in representing me in finding a publisher for my book. So let's get through this together, and then we'll celebrate."

Jennifer sat quietly, wringing her hands, as her friend drained her glass and rose to go. "Thank you for coming, Nancy," she said, hugging her friend, "and congratulations on the agent." She closed the door and leaned against it until an oven timer went off.

Fifty

JENNIFER was pacing anxiously when John walked through the garage door thirty minutes later, and she began to relate the conversation with Nancy before he could even pour himself a drink.

"I'll call Al Farnsworth in the morning," he said, after listening without interruption. "I'd call him now, but I'd like to think about this overnight. To be honest with you, babe, I've been so focused on trying to get my big case moving in the right direction again, I'd lost track of the time. That claim should have been paid out by now. You should have received the money…"

"You haven't talked to me about your business lately," she said, grateful for the segue, "and I've been reluctant to ask. Are there any new developments, with the doctors?" She had been holding her questions back, trying not to crowd him. But the more stress he carried, the more worried she became.

"I wish I could answer that question, but the truth of the matter is, I just don't know. They've stopped communicating with me."

Jennifer thought she detected a hint of desperation in his voice.

"Please don't give up on me, Jeni."

"That," she said, shaking her head, "I will never do."

Fifty-one

"**AL** Farnsworth, please. John Crouch calling," John said, in response to the receptionist's greeting.

"Mr. Farnsworth is on another line now. May I ask him to call you back, or would you prefer to hold?"

"I'll hold, thank you." He listened to the elevator music through his speaker while scrolling down through his inbox.

"John? I apologize for the wait."

"No problem, Al. Hey, listen. I just thought I'd follow up with you about the Harringtons' life insurance policy. It's been over two months since Jennifer signed the beneficiary claim form. And to be honest, she had a friend stop by yesterday with a report that disturbed her a little, something about a private investigator asking some questions about Dick's death."

"I've been meaning to call you about the insurance—sorry you had to learn about the delay like this. I didn't know about the PI, but I guess I should have expected it. From what I understand, a representative from the Mayo Foundation went to the insurance company with some concerns. Mayo is the other policy beneficiary, as you know. They're also the beneficiary of the rest of the Harringtons' estate, which, I might add, is much more valuable than the life insurance. So, it isn't that they're being greedy—at least I don't think that's it. They're a tight-knit community, and Dick never told their development people about making the change, so it raised some suspicion with them. Apparently, the insurance company agreed to investigate the matter, at their request."

"Suspicion…" said John, drawing the word out. "What kind of suspicion?"

"Oh, you know. The usual, I assume. Were the Harringtons of sound mind, were they under any pressure…"

"But you know the answers to those questions, Al. You were there. And at my suggestion."

"I know, John, and I'll tell them that, if they ask. So far, no one has contacted me. I know about this from the Mayo folks. The biggest eyebrow raiser, as I see it, is the short time between when the change was made and when the deaths occurred. We knew Shirley was sick, of course, but we certainly weren't expecting Dick to go like he did. I still can't believe it, to tell you the truth. Anyway, try not to worry about it, and let's just let things take their course. They will whether you worry or not.

"By the way, changing the subject now, my wife and I had dinner recently with one of your doctor clients and his wife. He asked if I knew you, and I said I did. He told me about the buy-sell/deferred comp plan you had proposed to his group, wanted my opinion. I told him I thought it made perfect sense."

"Thank you, Al. Thank you very much. Please call me if you hear any more about this investigation or the insurance."

"Will do. Bye now."

Fifty-two

"**YOU** have reached the Maricopa County medical examiner's office. We are experiencing an unusually high call volume. Please stay on the line, and someone will be with you shortly. Thank you."

Frank tapped his fingers on his desk and waited.

"Maricopa County medical examiner, how may we help you?"

"Deputy Frank Chavez calling for Dr. Riley."

"One moment, please."

"Ron Riley speaking."

"Ron, Frank Chavez, how's it going?"

"Not well, Sheriff, not well at all. Forecasters are predicting the hottest summer on record. Last year's heat wave was murder, literally. Homeless people dying on the street like flies. Social services trying to get them inside, but, you know, some of them just don't want to come in—they're paranoid, or they're hopped up on meth, or they're camped out in places where they can't be found, until it's too late. I've never seen anything like it. You made out okay in Fountain Hills, as I recall."

"Yeah, it was hot for sure, but not like Phoenix. Less pavement, fewer vehicles. I don't know how people can deny climate change, but that's a topic for another day. I know you're busy, so I'll get to the point. A few months ago, one of your guys met me out in Tonto Verde, a golf community east of north Scottsdale. An elderly doctor was found dead in his hot tub, by the maid, when she arrived in the morning. No sign of foul play, advanced age, and the guy was a widower with no family, so we saw no need for an autopsy. My bad, I guess. Turns out the deceased had a big life insurance policy, and the beneficiary had been changed shortly before his death. Apparently, the doctor and his wife, who died a few months prior to him, had known the new beneficiary less than a year when they made the change. The Mayo Foundation, the other beneficiary, has raised concerns with the insurance company. They've hired a private investigator, who has raised concerns with us. You know where I'm going with this…"

"Where's the body?"

"Hansen Desert Hills, Scottsdale."

Ron sighed. "Okay. Have you talked to the county attorney?"

"Filed a request to exhume yesterday. Just wanted to give you a heads up. The doctor was a prominent cardiologist, a lifer with the Mayo."

"I'll handle it personally. Sorry, Frank. These things happen. Hopefully no drama. I'll be in touch with what I learn."

"Thanks, Ron."

Fifty-three

GREG Thornburg walked briskly down the hallway toward the reception area. John Crouch sat on the edge of one of the sofas there, pretending to be interested in yesterday's copy of the *Wall Street Journal*. He rose quickly to shake the hand extended to him.

"Good to see you, John," said Greg. "Let's step into this conference room. Can I get you something to drink?"

"No thanks, I'm fine."

"Thank you for coming over on such short notice. You've been patient, very responsive to our numerous requests for more information, for revisions, and so on. The docs have dragged their feet, and we all apologize. I'm sorry, personally, for not returning your calls or responding to your emails. I should have kept you in the loop.

"But they've decided to go forward with the most recent version of your proposal. In fact—you'll love this—now they're in a hurry to get it done. They'll make themselves totally available for whatever you need. Apparently one of them had a scare over the weekend. A car passed him with oncoming traffic on a two-lane highway—almost ran him off into a ditch. Says his wife told him, then and there, she was leaving him if he didn't get this life insurance thing done. So where do we start?"

"That's great, Greg. Not about the near accident, of course. I'm glad everyone's okay. *Praise the Lord. Thank you, Jesus. We're actually going to get this thing done!*

"We have a mountain of paperwork to submit. We'll prepare what we can in-house, but then we'll need to sit down with each applicant for some personal questions, signatures and authorizations—that kind of thing. I assume you'll be signing on behalf of the corporation."

Greg nodded his assent, and John continued.

"Each applicant will need to be examined. Given the amount of insurance we're applying for, it will need to be an MD, not a paramedic. The older ones will need an EKG; some of our approved examiners have mobile units. We'll have as many of the exams as possible done right here at your office, if you like. They'll include a blood draw, so the docs will need to fast overnight.

"It'll take anywhere from six weeks to three months, maybe longer, to get all the policies issued. But we can bind the coverage for up to two million each with the first month's premium, once the exams are completed. That's at least a start. I'll have an invoice worked up for you.

"The insurance company will want to see the executed buy-sell agreement. I assume you'll be coordinating that, but let me know if I can help. We have a checklist that outlines all the steps I just mentioned, and a few more. I'll shoot it over to you. Any questions for now?"

"I think you've answered them, John. We'll just rely on you to guide us through the process. Thank you again for your patience."

John rose to go. "Thank *you*, Greg, for your confidence in me."

Fifty-four

"GREAT news, Jeni! We can break out that bottle of good champagne we've been saving. And you can start going through open houses this weekend—I know you love doing that. It's finally happening. I just got out of a meeting with Greg Thornburg. The doctors are ready to move. I was beginning to think this day would never come."

"Oh my God. Congratulations, honey! I'm not surprised, just happy. I can't wait to hear all about it. Where are you?"

"Shea and Palisades. Do you need me to pick anything up? I'll be going right by the store."

"Don't stop. I'll thaw out a couple of steaks and you can put them on the grill. This tuna casserole will keep. And don't get a ticket driving through the park. I hear the sheriff is out. Honey, I love you. I'm so proud of you. I'm so, so proud!"

Fifty-five

"**W**HAT the…" John exclaimed, as he swung into his driveway thirty minutes later. A black SUV from the Maricopa County sheriff's department was parked in front of the house. He slammed the car door and ran inside. "Jeni, are you all right? What's going on?"

"I'm fine, John." She smiled, wanly, from her seat on the edge of the sofa.

"Mr. Crouch, Deputy Frank Chavez," the uniformed officer said as he rose from the chair opposite the sofa. He extended his hand and John shook it.

"I was just having a visit with Mrs. Crouch about your friend, Dr. Harrington."

"Dick died three months ago…" John said.

"Yes, I'm aware of that. Some questions have come up surrounding the circumstances of his death. I wonder if you and Mrs. Crouch would mind coming to the station in Fountain Hills? It's across the parking lot from the River of Time Museum, just off the traffic circle, there at Avenue of the Fountains and La Montana. You can drive your car, and Mrs. Crouch can ride with me. We'll follow you."

"Yes, of course. I mean, no, of course we don't mind."

"And if you don't mind getting your passports out of the safe—Mrs. Crouch mentioned that's where you secure them."

"Yes, of course. Deputy Chavez, do I need to contact an attorney? I mean, am I, are we, in some kind of trouble?"

"Why don't we head on into town for now, and if you decide you need to make that call, I won't make it a problem for you."

"Yes, of course, excuse me."

John walked down the hallway and into their bedroom on shaky legs. As he fumbled with the keypad on the small home safe he kept on his side of the closet, he took a few deep breaths. His fingers were trembling so that he had to put the code in several times before he heard the familiar click. He removed the two small navy booklets and emerged from the bedroom, glancing back at the bed. So much for his plans for the evening. He'd imagined making love to Jeni after enjoying a flute of champagne on the patio. Instead, he would be backtracking through McDowell Mountain State Park, with Jennifer, and the sheriff, in his rear-view mirror.

Fifty-six

THROUGH the SUV windshield, Jennifer watched John pull into the Fountain Hills municipal complex and park his car near the entrance to the Town Hall, where the sheriff's office was located. Deputy Chavez took a vacant spot next to John's Audi, so that her car window was directly opposite his. She looked through the glass at him, seeing both love, and fear, in his eyes. He got out and locked his car, opening her door and helping her step down to the pavement. She held his hand as they followed the sheriff into the building. He led them through a set of locked doors into a vestibule, and finally into a reception area, where they sat in the chairs indicated. She looked up, curious, as another man in uniform entered the room.

"Mr. Crouch, Mrs. Crouch, this is Deputy Price. We are investigating what we believe to be the murder of Dr. Richard Harrington, and we'd like to ask you a few questions. You do not have to answer them, and you may call an attorney if you desire."

Jennifer looked at John, stunned. "Murder?" she said.

"Dick? Murdered?" echoed John.

"John, should we call the attorney you've been working with on the insurance?"

"He's not the right kind of attorney, Jeni." Then, speaking for them both, he said, "Deputy Chavez, my wife and I have nothing to hide. If our friend was murdered, we want to help you find the killer. We're happy to answer your questions."

"Thank you, Mr. Crouch. Please come with me. Mrs. Crouch, will you please go with Deputy Price?"

Jennifer followed the second officer through yet another set of doors, looking back over her shoulder at John until he was no longer visible.

Fifty-seven

"MRS. Crouch, please be seated. May I get you something to drink?"

"Water would be nice, thank you." She opened the plastic bottle he retrieved for her from a cabinet and took a sip. It was room temperature, and not very refreshing, but she was suddenly parched.

"Mrs. Crouch, we're sorry to bring you out this evening. I know you and Mr. Crouch want to get home to your dinner. Could you please tell me about your relationship to Dr. Harrington?"

Jennifer related the story of how they had met, of their developing friendship with the older couple, of Shirley's illness and death, and of their efforts to support Dick in his grief.

"You often provided meals to Dr. Harrington, is that correct?"

"Yes, I love to cook, and to share food with my friends."

"And if I understand correctly, Mrs. Crouch, you had prepared dinner for Dr. Harrington the night before he was found dead?"

"Yes, that's true. How did you know?"

"I believe you mentioned it to a group at your church." Jennifer shrank down in her chair, imagining her acquaintances being questioned about her.

"Yes."

"And what was the dinner you prepared?"

"Green chili chicken casserole, salad, and brownies." She didn't elaborate, suddenly struck by a desire to be as succinct as possible.

"That sounds delicious. What are the ingredients—in the casserole, I mean."

"Chicken, hominy, green chilies, ranch dressing, cheese."

"And did you deliver this dinner to Dr. Harrington?"

He already knows otherwise. "No, I had planned to, but my husband came home early from work that day, so I asked him to deliver the food."

"And did he return immediately, or did he have a visit with Dr. Harrington?"

"Dick didn't answer the front door, so he let himself in through the garage. We have the code for the Harringtons' keypad. He put the food in the refrigerator." But he didn't return home until about forty-five minutes later, she suddenly remembered. When he came in, he was in much better spirits than when he had left. An ominous thought crept into her brain. She shook her head in a visceral attempt to dislodge it.

"Mrs. Crouch, have you ever heard of thallium?"

"No, I haven't. What is it?"

"It's a poison, Mrs. Crouch. Hard to detect, but deadly, nonetheless. Traces of thallium have been discovered in Dr. Harrington's body."

Fifty-eight

"**HAVE** a seat, Mr. Crouch. May I get you a water?"

"Yes, thank you. Please, call me John."

"Do you have any idea why we've asked you to come in, John?"

"Obviously, it has to do with Dick Harrington's death, Deputy Chavez. We'll do anything we can to help. Dick was a good friend."

"Yes, he must have been, to want to leave you a million dollars."

"The money was actually left to my wife."

"Do you and Mrs. Crouch maintain separate bank accounts?"

"Well, no, but..."

"Your assets are shared, aren't they? I believe you moved here from California, is that correct? California is a community property state."

John nodded. "That's true."

"Is it safe to say that if your wife were to receive a million dollars, she would share the money with you?"

"Well, yes, of course. But the truth is, I don't have any need for the money, other than to make my wife happy."

"And what would that take, John? Making your wife happy, I mean."

"I…she…when we moved here there wasn't much on the market in the way of homes. We bought a condo, and Jennifer's happy enough with it, but I want her to have her dream house. I assume she'll use the insurance money the Harringtons left her to purchase a larger home, one with a view. My wife is a wonderful person, an excellent cook and a great hostess, but she's…a little insecure at times, thinks people care about social status, you know… and let's be honest, some people do."

"Yes, that's true. But you have a good income, don't you, John?"

"I do, but…"

"For a while there you weren't so sure, is that it?"

"Well, yes, but…"

"You were working on a big case, weren't you? With a group of doctors?"

"Yes. Fortunately, it's moving forward. The biggest premium I've ever brought in." *And the biggest production bonus I've ever earned.*

"What was the status of that case the day you took the dinner your wife had prepared over to the Harrington home?"

"I was afraid it might be dead," John said, then cringed at his choice of words.

"Tell me a little more about that day."

"I had a meeting scheduled with my clients in the afternoon. However, they cancelled at the last minute, something about one of the doctors having a sick kid. I left the office early. I was feeling down, depressed, actually. I thought the sick kid was a lousy excuse, that they were putting me off. I told Jennifer I thought I had lost the case."

"And?"

"She had made dinner for Dick Harrington and asked me to take it to him. When he didn't answer the door, I left it in the refrigerator like she told me to. Then, I drove my golf cart over to the park.

Tonto has its own back entrance. The sun was beginning to set, and it was beautiful. I just sat there for a while. I'm not religious, but I do believe in a higher power. Anyway, I began to feel calm, like everything would work out. And it has…the case, I mean, and hopefully being able to get my wife her dream house."

"And the next day your friend's body was discovered by his housekeeper. John, we believe that your friend Dick Harrington was poisoned, and we have reason to suspect that you or your wife might possibly have had something to do with it. We're sure to have more questions for you in the next few days, so you'll want to stay close to home. For now, you're free to go."

Fifty-nine

"FRANK, what the heck, are you crazy?"

"Excuse me, who's calling?"

"Nancy, Nancy Scott. You gave me your mobile number. And I'm sorry, of course you're not crazy, I apologize for saying that, it's very disrespectful of me. But you have the wrong idea about the Crouches. They didn't kill Dick Harrington. They loved him! And now they're stuck at home, under a cloud of suspicion. For heaven's sake! John needs to be at the office. There's a big case he's been working on for months now. He can't afford to lose it. I don't understand what's going on…"

"Nancy, I appreciate your concern for your friends, and to be clear, they aren't under arrest. No charges have been filed. I'm sure you understand I'm not at liberty to discuss the details of a case under investigation."

"But I was there with you the day Dick Harrington's body was discovered!"

Frank considered things for a moment. Maybe there was a role for Nancy in his investigation.

"Why don't you come into Fountain Hills, and we'll talk," he said.

"I'll be there in twenty minutes."

Frank smiled. "If you're here in twenty minutes, you're driving too fast."

"Got it. I'll be there as quickly as I can be, driving the speed limit."

"I'll see you soon."

Sixty

"**NANCY** Scott to see Deputy Chavez."

"Come in, Ms. Scott," said the receptionist. "The sheriff is expecting you. May I get you a bottle of water? You seem out of breath."

"That'd be great," said Nancy, panting. "I jogged here—had to park three blocks away. It's the Farmers' Market this morning, and it's hot out there." She went down the hall, pausing at Frank's open office door, where she saw that he sat behind his desk. A uniformed deputy sat across from him in one of the two guest chairs.

Frank waved her into the room. "It's nice to see you again, Nancy," he said, rising and extending his hand. "Meet Deputy Price."

"Nice to meet you, Ms. Scott. Call me Dennis."

She slid into the vacant chair and opened her water bottle. "Likewise. And please, call me Nancy." She took the clean-cut young man sitting next to her to be about thirty, if that. He probably grew up on Law & Order and always wanted to be a cop; he looked like he belonged in uniform.

"Dennis is assisting my investigation into the murder of Dr. Harrington," said Frank. Turning to his deputy, he added, "Nancy was with me at Dr. Harrington's home the morning his body was discovered. She's good friends with the Crouches." Turning back to Nancy, he asked, "So what makes you so sure neither John nor Jennifer Crouch was involved in Dr. Harrington's murder?"

She took a long drink of water before answering. "First of all, Frank, they're not that kind of people. I know them, and more importantly, I know people. Second, how did this death go from being classified as 'natural causes' to 'homicide'? You yourself said…" she paused to take another drink.

"Yes, I know," said Frank. "Are you familiar with a substance called thallium sulphate?"

"Duh, Agatha Christie's favorite murder weapon. What are you saying, Frank? Thallium has been banned in the U.S. for decades."

"That's true. But the coroner found traces of it in Richard Harrington's body. Look, your friends seem like nice people, and Dennis and I are committed to conducting a thorough and fair investigation. We're not rushing to conclusions. But for now, the Crouches are our best suspects, our only suspects, to be honest with you. They had motive, and they had opportunity."

"That's purely circumstantial, and how in the world would either of them have gotten hold of thallium?"

"We're not sure about that yet. Maybe the doctor had a very old box of rat poison in his garage. Look, we're going to keep exploring this from every angle. We just need to be sure the Crouches don't take off for Mexico in the meantime. Why don't you help us out by being our eyes and ears in the Tonto community. Don't misunderstand me, I'm not asking you to spy on your friends. But someone knows something—someone always does. And you've told me that you're a sleuth at heart."

"Okay…I guess I could do that." Warming to the idea, she added, "I'll do anything I can to help clear my friends."

"That's the spirit," said Frank.

"In return, I have a favor to ask. Could we please try to keep this quiet? Jennifer, well, she cares a lot about what people think. And John has worked so hard to establish his professional reputation here."

"I can't make any promises in that regard, but we're certainly not looking to publicize this. Your friends are innocent until proven guilty, just like anyone else, and we'll do what we can to protect their reputations in the meantime. Call me if you come up with any ideas."

"Thank you, Frank," she said, rising to leave. "It's nice meeting you, Dennis."

She thanked the receptionist again for the water and left the building, walking briskly past the produce stands that lined the Avenue of the Fountains on the way back to her car.

Sixty-one

"HEY, Nancy." Jennifer answered the phone right away. She sounded glum. Not that Nancy blamed her. Cabin fever must be setting in.

"Good morning. I'm in town, stopping at Safeway. What can I pick up for you?"

"White wine, please."

"Will do, anything else?"

"Maybe some pre-washed salad greens? A frozen pizza? I don't know, I have no idea how long I'm going to be a prisoner in my own home. That's not fair. I could go out. But I don't want to take a chance on Frank coming after me in the Tonto clubhouse! John, too. He's afraid to go to the office, and he needs to be there."

"Yeah, well, we're going to work on that. I'll drop by my house and put stuff in the fridge, then head over to your place and we can talk."

"Thanks, Nancy. You're the best."

Sixty-two

"BUENO, hello."

"Rosario Gonzales?

"Sí."

"Me llamo Dennis Price, deputado en Fountain Hills. No estás en problemas, pero necesito habla contigo." Thank goodness his mother had insisted he take Spanish in high school, he thought, though his proficiency level often left him feeling like a first grader. "Está bien?"

"Sí…"

"¿Limpiaste el garaje de los Harringtons hace tres meses?"

"No, un amigo mío limpiaste. Juan Silva. Pero, él ha sido deportado, a Venezuela."

"Oh, crap," the deputy exclaimed, smacking his forehead, then recovering his composure. "Lo siento mucho, Rosario. ¿Qué hizo Juan con el contenido del garaje?"

"Los llevó al basurero, Señor Price." *The dump. Double crap.*

"Veo, veo. Muchas gracias por su tiempo, Rosario. Adiós."

"Adiós, goodbye."

Sixty-three

"WHAT'S up, Price, any luck?"

"Nah, the housekeeper got an illegal from Venezuela to clean the doctor's garage out, but the guy got sent back."

"Undocumented, Price, not illegal. People are not illegal."

"Sorry." His boss could be so prickly when it came to these migrants.

"Look, you hold down the fort while I head over to Rio Verde. We've got an apparent suicide by gunshot. The medical examiner's guy is meeting me there. I always thought of the Verdes as being kind of sleepy. Not lately."

Sixty-four

"**THANK** you for coming, and thank you for the groceries and the wine," said Jennifer. "Let's have a glass now; it's five o'clock somewhere. I'm going a little crazy here. I've worked every crossword puzzle in the house; I'm starting on the jigsaws now. I need a workout in the worst way, but I'm embarrassed to go to the fitness center, scared I'll see someone who, you know, knows about this. Maybe we could go for a walk early tomorrow morning, when it's cool."

She waved down the hallway. "John's in his office, waiting for a criminal defense lawyer to return his call, and trying to stay on top of business. Nancy, you do know I'm innocent, don't you?"

"Of course, I know that. And John, too. We just need to figure out who killed your friend." Nancy pulled a pencil and notepad from her purse and took a sip from the glass Jennifer handed her. "Sit down and put on your Dr. Watson hat. I'll be Sherlock."

Jennifer couldn't help laughing at this suggestion, but soon realized her friend was serious.

"Did the Harringtons have any enemies? Anyone who would want to see Dr. Harrington dead?"

Jennifer shook her head. "No, I can't imagine that. They were the nicest people you've ever met, or, in your case, that you never met. I wish you *had* met them."

"Me too. But back to the question. Dr. Harrington had been a heart surgeon, right? What if he made a mistake, accidentally did something that resulted in a death. Maybe someone's spouse or, God forbid, their child."

"I guess that's possible," Jennifer said, "but it seems unlikely. I know he was highly respected in his field."

"I know. No family, right? Their only son died young. No grandkids they didn't know they had…"

"I never thought about that. I think they would have been thrilled to learn they had a grandchild. But no, I don't think that's possible."

"What about the housekeeper? Were you around her much?"

"She was very quiet, always in the background, and doesn't speak much English. She worked for them a long time. She was so kind to Shirley during her illness, and to Dick, after Shirley died. And to me when I came to visit. The Harringtons' executor told John I could go over to the house and select some personal things. I wanted a picture, and Rosario showed me some to choose from. Would you like to see it?"

Nancy nodded.

Jennifer went into the bedroom and returned with a framed black and white photo, one obviously taken by a professional. A petite, dark-haired Shirley with a short bob and slightly arched eyebrows sat holding a light-haired child of about three who wore a Scandinavian-style sweater. A handsome younger version of Dick, with thick, wavy hair, towered over them. All three looked toward the unseen camera, their natural smiles revealing beautiful, straight teeth. The picture could have been an advertisement for a dentist, or for a hair salon, or for a manufacturer of children's sweaters. Nancy studied it.

"What a perfect family," she murmured. "Who could have imagined…"

Jennifer wiped a tear from her eye.

Sixty-five

FRANK pulled up in front of a tile-roofed stucco home with mature landscaping in the golf community of Rio Verde. This community had been developed first, by the same family that built Tonto Verde directly to the north of it, and featured tall palms and Spanish-style architecture throughout. Both Verdes were virtually crime-free, with Rio reporting an occasional burglary due to easier access and multiple exits. A man Frank guessed might be in his late seventies answered the door and solemnly pointed him toward one of three bedrooms. He braced himself. People who took their own lives with a gun were not leaving anything to chance. He stood in the doorway and stared at the body on the bed, eyes and mouth wide open in a balding head that lay on a blood-soaked pillow. A small handgun rested on its chest. He turned and walked back to the living room.

"Was anyone here at the time?" he asked.

"His wife, Linda. She's next door with my wife. We're close friends, built here the same year, mid- eighties. Came out from Wisconsin part-time, then moved here full-time when we retired. Attended each other's kids' weddings, took cruises together, that kind of friends."

"I'm sorry for your loss. His name was Tom Scoggin, is that correct?" Frank had done a reverse address lookup on his way out.

"That right. I'm Bill. Bill Grimmel."

"Nice to meet you, Mr. Grimmel. Deputy Chavez." He offered his hand. "You made the call. Stated it was a suicide, and it certainly appears to be. Did Mr. Scoggin leave a note?"

Bill Grimmel pointed to a sheet of paper on the dining room table. The sheriff walked to it and bent to read the note, written in blue ink on letterhead from what appeared to be a law firm with a Milwaukee address. The writing was legible, but barely.

To my beloved wife and children: I cannot bear to put you through what I know lies ahead for me. To be more honest, I can't bear to go through it myself. Being diagnosed with ALS is a death sentence. With no known cure and no guarantee of when I might be released, I'm taking matters into my own hands. Please forgive me for doing what I feel I must do. I love you so much. Tom, Dad

ALS. Amyotrophic Lateral Sclerosis, sometimes referred to as Lou Gehrig's Disease, after the famous Yankee first baseman who died from it at age thirty-eight. From what Frank had heard, he wasn't sure he wouldn't be tempted to take his own life with a diagnosis of ALS. Of course, as a practicing Catholic, he could never do that. His religion taught that each life is the property of God, and to take one's own life goes against God. Still, if the Arizona legislature ever passed a bill allowing for physician-assisted death, he wouldn't be totally opposed to it. Anything to keep a loved one from having to live with the memory of the grim scene down the hall.

"This is your friend's handwriting?"

Bill nodded. "Linda found it on his desk."

"Someone from the medical examiner's office is on the way out to certify the cause of death. They're coming from downtown. They should be here before long, depending on traffic. You may want to help Mrs. Scoggin call the funeral home to pick up the body afterward. I assume she's not planning to stay here tonight. I can give you the names of a couple of companies that clean up after this kind of thing. Most homeowners' policies pay for it. Mind if I look around?"

Frank walked through the house. It was clean and orderly, if somewhat overcrowded with possessions from many years' worth of accumulation. Framed photographs of smiling families stood on almost every surface—children, grandchildren, and great-grandchildren, Frank assumed. Finger paintings signed "To Nana and Papa" covered the refrigerator. Frank suddenly felt an acute longing for his own family.

"I think I'll wait in the car." He closed the front door, pulling a handkerchief from his pocket and pressing it to his eyes.

Sixty-six

ON the way back to Fountain Hills Frank dictated into his mobile phone, "Call Maria Chavez."

"Frank?" his sister whispered into the phone, "is everyone okay?"

"Everyone's fine, but I need to talk to you."

"I'm observing a surgery right now. I'll call you back in about fifteen minutes."

When Maria returned his call Frank was pulling into the parking lot at the station. He maneuvered into an empty space and turned off the engine, leaving the air conditioner running.

"What do you know about thallium?" he dove in, without pleasantries.

Maria laughed. "Are those kangaroo rats getting in under your foundation again?"

"This is serious, Sis. Do they have it at the Mayo?"

"You *sound* serious. The answer to your question is probably 'yes'. That said, substances in the Mayo vault are better protected than the gold at Fort Knox."

"But a long-term and highly respected Mayo physician could get into that vault, right?"

"Maybe. There's a security officer that ID's people, checks them in and out. Why are you asking me about this?"

"It's a hunch I'm following up on, that's all. Look, I need some information. Can you go into your patient database and tell me who Richard Harrington's primary care doctor was? I assume he saw one of his colleagues. If it's a problem, just say so. I don't want to get you into trouble. I can always come over with a warrant."

"I'll call you back as soon as I can," she said.

Sixty-seven

FRANK sat, deep in thought, at his desk, when his mobile displayed a number that he had added to his contacts. "You got something for me, Detective Scott?"

"Maybe. And thank you for the promotion," Nancy said. "Here's what I have. Jennifer told me that Dr. Harrington had become quite clumsy—my words, not hers—dropping his wine glass at dinner, having trouble holding on to his golf clubs, that kind of thing. It could have just been a combination of age and grief; or, he could have been developing some kind of a neurological disorder."

"I know. I mean, I didn't know, but I'm wondering…"

"But that doesn't explain the thallium poisoning," Nancy said, sounding impatient.

"It may."

"Huh?"

Frank didn't have time to explain. "Listen, I'm waiting for a callback from Richard Harrington's doctor. Depending on what

I learn, I may be heading over to the Mayo. I'll be in touch. And Nancy, thank you."

"You're welcome. Anything to help my friends get their life back."

Sixty-eight

JENNIFER padded to the front door in her bare feet when the bell rang, expecting the grocery delivery she had ordered online. Instead, Gretchen Yarborough stood on the welcome mat, holding a foil-covered plate.

"May I come in?"

"Of course, Gretchen. How nice to see you. Please sit down." Jennifer accepted the plate, lifting the foil to reveal a small coffee cake, still warm from the oven and smelling of cinnamon. "May I make a pot of tea? This smells too good not to taste right now."

"Please don't go to any trouble. Is John here?"

"It's no trouble at all, and, yes, John's in his office," said Jennifer, as she filled the kettle on the stove and took three small plates from the cupboard. She wasn't sure how to act. Obviously, Gretchen had heard about their situation. Should she pretend it was no big thing? A simple misunderstanding? Remembering the rewards she'd reaped—not the money, but the emotional rewards—by being totally herself with Shirley, she decided that being open and honest about it was her best way forward.

"Thank you for coming," she said, when they were settled. "I'm going…we're going…through a difficult time."

"I know. I'll be direct. Gary and I want you to know that *we* know you had nothing to do with Dick's death. Whatever happens, we want you to know that."

"Thank you, Gretchen. I'm sorry that the word is out that Dick's death is being investigated as a murder, with us as the suspects."

"You can't keep a secret in Tonto, Jennifer." She added gently, "You must have learned that by now."

"Do people know…everything?"

"You mean about the insurance? Yes."

Jennifer felt her face burn, as tears gathered and spilled over, running down her cheeks. Gretchen handed her a tissue from her purse.

"Look, I don't know what happened, but I do know Dick and Shirley Harrington cared deeply for you. That's why, I assume, they wanted to give you something.

"During my career in hospice I often asked dying people if they had any regrets. When Shirley was ill, and I visited her, I asked her that question. It was bold of me, because no one had said she was dying, but to be honest, I had a sense she was not going to recover. She told me she regretted keeping the memory of her son bottled up all these years, and that talking to you had helped her resolve that. Your ability to listen was a gift, *is* a gift."

The kettle whistled, and Jennifer rose to pour boiling water over loose leaves in a china pot. She brought it to the coffee table on a tray that held a dish of lemon slices, a bowl of sugar cubes, and a small pitcher of milk. After waiting a few minutes, she used a strainer to pour the steeped tea into two delicate cups, handing one of them, on a saucer, to Gretchen.

"Earl Grey," she told her guest. "Please add whatever you like. I'm going to slip John a slice of cake."

"This is elegant, very proper."

"Actually, I'm channeling Shirley." Jennifer smiled wistfully as she cut another slice of the coffee cake. "Prior to meeting her, it was tea bags or K-cups for me."

"She was an elegant influencer, wasn't she?"

"She was. And if—I mean, when—we get out of this predicament, I intend to do something meaningful to honor her memory. Excuse me just a minute."

Jennifer silently turned the knob of her husband's office door and stepped inside. He sat at his desk, his head in his hands. She went to him, setting the cake down and touching his shoulder. "Honey, what is it?" she said. He turned to look into her eyes.

"I'm ruined, Jeni. We're ruined. I just had a call from James McDougal. Somehow, he got wind of the investigation. He was nice enough, sympathetic even, but said the firm didn't want this kind of publicity. He and one of the other associates are taking over the case with the docs, and anything else I've got in the works. I pleaded with him—he knows how much I have invested in it—but he reminded me of the terms of my contract. The business is theirs."

Jennifer's mind raced from one disaster to the next. Her heart was beating so hard she thought it might burst through her chest. When she heard the doorbell ring, it sounded like it was a million miles away.

"Groceries," she said, without expression.

She moved like a sleepwalker toward the door, but when she opened it, instead of the Instacart delivery person she expected to see, she found herself looking up at the sheriff.

"May I come in?" he asked.

"Of course, Deputy Chavez," she said, indicating a seat across from where she and Gretchen had been sitting side by side. "This is Gretchen Yarborough. She and her husband were also friends of the Harringtons."

The sheriff tipped his hat. "Yes, I believe we met at Dr. Harrington's home the morning his body was discovered. It's nice to see you again, Mrs. Yarborough."

John emerged from his office. "Deputy Chavez? Any update?"

Gretchen rose to leave, but the sheriff motioned her to stay. Jennifer offered him a cup of tea, which he declined.

"I have news for all of you, about your deceased friend," he began, as John sat down on the arm of the sofa next to Jennifer, resting his hand on her shoulder.

The sheriff continued, "It seems Dr. Harrington had been diagnosed with Parkinson's."

"I knew it," whispered Gretchen.

"He was apparently in the middle stages of the disease and implored his doctor to keep silent. There was only the briefest documentation in his file."

"But why would he do that? And how does this relate to the poison in his system?" John asked.

Jennifer, too, was struggling to process this information in a way that made sense.

"Self-administered, we now believe."

Gretchen gasped. "Why didn't he tell us he was sick? We could have helped him negotiate the support he needed. Verdes Cares provides all kinds of help for people with Parkinson's. Dick knew that. He'd served on the board." She shook her head.

"My guess is he didn't want to be a burden to his friends," said the sheriff, "and he had no family."

"But we were his family," Jennifer said, swallowing a lump of sadness.

"But," John said, "he didn't leave a note. Did he mean for us to wonder?"

The sheriff shook his head. "My guess, and again, it's only a guess, is that the doctor assumed his death would be ruled a natural one, which it was, until the insurance company got involved. He knew that thallium is difficult to detect. He also knew that older people are advised not to sit too long in the spa. He arranged his death to look like a natural event, rather than a death by suicide. God only knows why he chose to handle it this way."

"Actually," Jennifer said, "I have an idea why." She felt everyone's eyes on her and continued, tentatively. "It may have been for religious reasons."

"But Dick was Lutheran," Gretchen said, frowning.

"But reared Catholic," said Jennifer, "in the day when suicide was considered a mortal sin. He stepped away from his faith; "lapsed" is how they refer to it. Shirley convinced him to experience her family's faith and brought him into the Lutheran fold. She told me all about it."

Jennifer jumped as the front door slammed open.

"Did you tell them, Frank?" Nancy Scott burst into the room, breathless, as usual. She rushed to the sofa and embraced both Jennifer and John in a group hug. "You're in the clear! There *was* no murder."

At this point the sheriff rose, taking the Crouches' passports from his pocket and placing them on the coffee table. Jennifer began to cry.

"Thank you, Deputy Chavez," said John, awash with relief, rising to shake the sheriff's hand. "We're going to be needing those."

Sixty-nine

"A penny for your thoughts." John reached for his wife's hand, gazing into her eyes while gently caressing her fingers. She shuddered slightly, a small wave of pleasure making its way from her fingertips to her bare toes. They were cruising the Rhone between Lyon and Avignon, the sun setting slowly over a sea of brilliant red poppies swaying in a gentle breeze.

"My thoughts are changing," she said, giving him a demure smile.

"How so?" He raised her fingers to his lips.

"I *had* been contemplating how I'm going to spend the second half of my life. Now I'm simply wondering whether we have time to make love before our assigned seating."

"Perhaps we should take up the matter of your future later, over a nightcap," he suggested, leading her into their cabin, leaving two half-filled glasses on the balcony table. "And don't worry about the other," he said, as he gently positioned her on the luxurious down-comforted bed. "At most we'll miss the appetizer course."

Seventy

"**GREAT** news!" Nancy greeted them when they arrived at their table, their untouched salad plates having just been removed.

"Sorry to be late," Jennifer said, hoping her flushed face didn't give them away. Ben rose to pull her chair from the table while his wife continued to speak with more than her usual exuberance.

"The cruise director has promised to put me on the schedule for a book talk, and my publisher has committed to transporting a box of books here in time for it—hot off the press! Cheers!"

The four of them raised their glasses, now filled with the champagne Ben had poured.

"To friendship, and to your success, Nancy," said John.

"And to yours," Ben added. "I understand that piece of business you've been working on for months is finally placed. That's cause for celebration."

"Thank you," said John, stealing a sideways glance at his wife. "We have a lot to be grateful for. It's been quite a year."

Jennifer beamed at her husband. "Santé," she said, raising her glass again, first in the direction of her husband, and then to her friends, as their dinner plates were placed on the table by their servers.

"My steak looks perfect," said Nancy, cutting into her filet mignon.

The sommelier returned with a bottle of Bordeaux that had been breathing on a sideboard. He poured a small amount for Ben to taste, then poured for the others, as the conversation fell into a contented lull, punctuated by the clinking of silverware against china.

As the table was cleared and the last of the wine poured out, Nancy said, "Jennifer, you're very quiet tonight. What's on your mind?"

"Is this a rhetorical question, or do you really want to know?" Jennifer loved being able to banter with Nancy. This aspect of friendship was new to her.

"Of course, I want to know!" said Nancy, manifesting what Jennifer had recently dubbed her "million-dollar smile".

"In that case, I'll tell you," said Jennifer. "You know how John and I have talked about moving to a larger home with a view of the mountains—a house where we could entertain more people, more elaborately?"

Everyone nodded.

"Well, now we can, with my inheritance, and John's bonus and all."

"That's wonderful!" said Nancy.

"Cheers!" said Ben, raising his glass.

Jennifer smiled. "But now I'm not so sure. I mean, I'd still like to be able to host a big party on occasion, but we have that beautiful clubhouse, don't we? I guess I'm having second thoughts about how much happier a move would really make me. I mean, what difference does the size of my house make? Does it matter to anyone who matters to me? Who am I trying to impress, anyway?"

No one spoke, but Jennifer caught the glimmer of love shining in John's eyes.

"I know people upgrade their living situation for all kinds of reasons—to accommodate visiting children and grandchildren for one. Sadly, that's not our situation. So, I'm thinking I'd like to do something more meaningful with this money, not for recognition, but to demonstrate my life has a purpose. I've thought about going to college—don't laugh—and getting a degree in psychology, or maybe social work. But four years of attending classes and taking exams? It's a little late for that.

"I've been told by more than one person that I'm a good listener, and I'm wondering, assuming it's true, what can I do with that gift? Well, there you have it—you may want to think twice before asking next time."

It had become quiet, and Jennifer suddenly realized their party of four was the only one left in the ship's elegant dining room. Even the captain had slipped out.

Nancy broke the silence. "You know what?"

Jennifer waited for her to go on.

"Whatever it is you're meant to do, it's going to come to you. Now that you're open to it, the idea will present itself. Be patient. Trust the universe. Trust yourself."

Jennifer nodded. *Yes.*

Epilogue

THE private dining room in the Tonto Verde clubhouse was humming with conversation and laughter as Jennifer, feeling beautiful in a chartreuse shantung pantsuit, stepped forward to test the microphone. Around her neck hung a delicate gold chain with a diamond-encrusted heart, a gift from John in honor of the occasion.

"Good evening, everyone," said Jennifer, beaming with confidence. As the room quieted, she continued. "Good evening, and thank you so much for coming. I'm not much for public speaking, but the subject at hand is so near and dear to my heart that I'm only a little bit nervous."

Everyone smiled, and she basked in their approval.

"Tonight marks the culmination of eleven months of brainstorming, planning, and fundraising—and a lot of praying." Jennifer gave a little laugh, and turned to where she knew Pastor Jean was standing, next to John.

"Thanks to you, Harrington House is happening. It will be so much more than just a building; however, I do want to thank our wonderful architect, Ben Witkowski." She paused while her audience clapped for Ben. "We break ground tomorrow at noon, in our fantastic location in the civic center in Fountain Hills. Please check out Ben's renderings tonight and ask him to give you a preliminary virtual tour."

Another round of applause went up, encouraging her on. Tears pricked at her eyes. *Hold it together, Jennifer. You've got a long way to go.*

"This is a dream come true for me, an idea becoming a reality, through the thoughtful insights of many people from diverse professional backgrounds. Harrington House will be a gathering place—a listening place—a place for one-on-one conversations, for group dialogues, and for community forums.

"It will be a safe place for teens to find a trained and caring adult to help them navigate the difficult and unique challenges they face in today's world. This is my own personal passion, and a way that I hope to plug in. It will be a place for parents to build communication skills, for partners to strengthen relationships, and for those who are grieving to find support.

"It will be a place for training people in the art of active listening, which we know helps to build trust, promote understanding, and deepen personal connections. Listening to each other is the way we develop collaborative thinking and consensus building, and learn to value viewpoints different from our own.

"One of our program goals is to bring in speakers who represent different sides of an issue, kind of like a town hall meeting, allowing them to model respectful listening. So often these days, even when we agree on what our problems are, we have such divergent opinions about how to approach them that we devolve into name-calling and personal criticism. This is not healthy for our society.

"As most of you know, my husband, John, and I, became close friends with Dick and Shirley Harrington. They were a devoted couple—devoted to each other, and to their community. They died within six months of one another. The Harringtons had endured a tragedy in their younger years, the loss of their only son, Richie. When they died, they had no surviving family.

"They left me a generous financial gift, which I imagine they expected John and I would use to purchase a larger home here in Tonto Verde. They had heard us talk about wanting to do that. But when we had the freedom and the funds to take that step, I realized that, for me, it isn't our house, or even the spectacular beauty of our desert, that make Tonto Verde such a special place to live. It's the people."

Another round of applause broke out, and Jennifer nodded at the crowd.

"I can see that many of your glasses are empty, and I'm ready for a glass of chardonnay myself," she said, after the room had quieted again. "Let me recognize and thank a few people, and then we can mix and mingle, and enjoy the beautiful buffet prepared by our wonderful chefs. If you can, please hold your applause.

"First and foremost, thank you, John Crouch." She sent a dazzling smile in her husband's direction. "This man is my soulmate, my biggest fan, and the love of my life.

"I want to thank his firm, McDougal Partners. In addition to giving John a great business opportunity, the company has agreed to match our personal one-million-dollar investment in Harrington House with another million. Thank you, James and Steve.

"The doctors and staff at the Mayo Clinic, both in Minnesota and here in Arizona, were like a big, extended family to Dick and

Shirley. Some of them are here tonight. The Mayo Foundation has offered to donate a third one-million-dollar check. Perhaps even more importantly, the clinic has agreed to partner with us in designing and providing critical programming to help meet the needs of the East Valley.

"And thanks to each of you for your generous contributions and your pledges of ongoing support. As they say, 'it takes a village.'" At this point, the room erupted in applause.

"Thank you. Thank you so much. We're almost there!

"My friend and former employer, attorney Maryann Jamison, has agreed to leave the corporate life in Los Angeles and relocate to Fountain Hills, with her husband and their two sons, to serve as Executive Director for Harrington House. We could not have found a better advocate for our cause.

"I also want to recognize the mayor of Fountain Hills. Stephanie has been a dream to work with, helping to shepherd us through zoning, and the like. Thank you, Madame Mayor.

"Sheriff's deputy Frank Chavez is one of those special people who strives to make life better every day, for everyone he meets. We are all lucky to have this man and his team protecting and promoting our community, and I thank him and his family for being here tonight.

"Please plan to attend tomorrow's groundbreaking, which will be blessed by a spiritual leader from the McDowell Yavapai Nation, and by our own Pastor Jean. All are invited, so help us spread the word. And now, please enjoy yourselves, and each other."

After more applause, and many congratulations, Jennifer managed to make her way to one of the high-top bistro tables, where Nancy and Gretchen stood waiting for her. She hugged her friends, and eagerly accepted the glass of wine Nancy pressed into her hand.

"I'm sorry," she said. "I forgot to thank the two of you, for always believing in me."

"We forgive you," Nancy grinned. "By the way, you were amazing."

Jennifer caught John's gaze across the room and held it. Later, she planned to thank him appropriately for the necklace. And for everything else.

Deputy Frank Chavez stood at the back of the room next to the rear entrance, where he had waited for his sister to arrive. "I thought June was coming with you," he whispered, as Jennifer concluded her remarks.

"She was," Maria whispered back, "but something awful happened to her at a bar in Scottsdale last night. Step outside with me and I'll tell you about it."

Coming in 2025,
A Murder at Rancho Manana,
next in the Saguaro series.

Acknowledgements

MY husband, Andy, suggested the prologue for *The Tonto Two-Step*, and over the course of eighteen months, I wrote a book to go with it. He listened patiently while I fleshed out plotlines and created characters, and he read and re-read scenes that had sometimes changed by only a word. He is a true partner in everything that means anything in my life.

My editor, Eva Fox Mate of Gemini Writer's Studio, is a consummate professional, and a friend. She is also the organizer of our "writing sprints" which are the only way I would ever complete a manuscript. My fellow sprinters, Ellen Fisher and Joel Johnson, encourage and enliven me, and I look forward to seeing them—virtually—most Wednesday and Friday mornings.

The fifteen women (including Ellen) who attended the Christina Baker Kline & Paula McLain Foreward Writing Retreat in Chamonix-Mont-Blanc are accomplished writers, and helped me to polish some of the remaining rough edges of my manuscript.

Veronica Yager, and the staff at Journey Bound Publishing, were able to turn this project around in record time; I appreciate their willingness to go above and beyond. Michael Gallagher is a talented artist, photographer, and framer in Fountain Hills, the first and only person I asked for a cover photo. Gabrielle Col worked her magic to make me look like an author.

I'm grateful to the Maricopa County sheriff's deputy who allowed me to spend a morning with her. She and her colleagues truly care for the constituents they serve.

Thank you, Jan Netting, for sharing your insurance expertise.

The story I have told here is a product of my imagination. But Tonto Verde is a real community, located in Rio Verde, Arizona. It is populated by accomplished and compassionate people, and Andy and I are thrilled to be a part of it. We're grateful to Dick and Paula, to Judith and Jackson, to Mac and Mondi, to Maria Elena and Tom, and to Cindy, for making it happen.

Sherry Hester Kenney